KONDI'S SECRET

Mysteries in Malawi, Book 3

Sylvia Stewart

CHAPTER 1

"It's just my luck to get caught in a thunderstorm," Kondi Chisale grumbled. Rain lashed against her and a blast of wind made her stagger onto the tarred surface of Malawi's M1 highway. She glanced left then right, looking for a break in traffic. Cars and lorries carrying goods to and from Lilongwe, the capitol city, glistened with rainwater as they flashed by. Their lights reflected on every falling drop and on the sheet of water streaming down the macadam surface.

Why couldn't I have been assigned to the early morning school period? I would have liked a morning schedule much better. And anyway, then I would have been home and dry instead of standing in this storm. But, no, I drew the three to seven thirty period. So here I am, soaking wet, with a broken umbrella and shoes sucked off my feet in the mud!

With one hand she shook the umbrella with its sagging, dripping ribs, and with the other hand she shook her muddy shoes. She pushed the book bag hanging over her shoulder to her back as she prepared to cross. *I hope at least my books keep dry in the plastic wrapping.*

She checked again, left and right, but traffic still streamed by, a crocodile of vehicles winding into the distance in each direction.

She shook her head. Raindrops sprang from the braid ends framing her face, hitting her nose and splashing in her eyes. The gathering gloom made it difficult to accurately measure the distance between the on-coming cars.

She looked across to where firelight gleamed through the doorway of her mother's cookhouse. "It's so near," she muttered in disgust, "yet so far!"

Something moved at the opposite edge of the highway near their home. Kezo, her baby brother, stood dabbling a long stick in a torrent of filthy water rushing down the deep roadside ditch that emptied into the river at the bottom of their hill. Fear clutched her heart so tightly she could hardly breathe.

Now what was he doing there? He was only three years old. Once Kezo was put to bed, he rarely woke until morning. He should be already asleep inside the house. Thunder must have wakened him.

"Kezo!" she shouted. Her voice sounded no louder than a whisper in the downpour's din, the rush of tires on flooded pavement and the surge of the torrent in the gutters. Another crack of thunder boomed overhead. "Kezo!" she shook the broken umbrella to catch his attention. "Get back!"

He heard her then. As the vehicles whizzed between them, Kondi saw him smile and he looked around for her as a happy expression crossed his baby face, streaming with rainwater. A flash of lightning whitened the plumpness of his cheeks and glimmered over his chubby arms.

"No, Kezo!" Kondi gestured desperately for him to go to the open kitchen door behind him. Kezo's smile beamed on. He jabbered something she couldn't hear. Instead of turning back toward the cookhouse and his mother, he took one step toward his sister, the water-filled gutter, and the dangerous thoroughfare.

"Kezo! Go back!" she yelled, pointing her umbrella again to the cookhouse and safety. She looked back and forth, searching for even a small break in the flow of cars and trucks.

"No, Kezo! Not this way! Go back! Go to Mai!" Her screams drowned in the roar of the stormy night. She saw him step forward again and slip on the sodden ditch bank, pitching him toward the raging, muddy water. He lost his stick. His arms whipped out trying to grab hold of something— anything—to save himself. Then he seemed to slide in slow motion down the bank. He disappeared under the leaping waves of ditchwater.

A frightening memory flashed through her mind of the day Kezo was born. She'd been seated under peach trees in the hospital *bwalo* warming her back in the weak sunshine. Suddenly, a black cloud blotted out the sunlight. An icy wind sprang up. The peach trees near the doorway began writhing, seeming to be a reflection her mother's agony in childbirth. Gusts snatched pink peach blossoms from the branches, bruising them into the dips and hollows streaking the ground, and flung them over the bank into every furrow that dropped into the Rift Valley several hundred feet below. She remembered thinking: 'Will my mother's baby live?'

Now, a moment of blind panic seized her again and the same frightening question clutched her heart, 'Will Kezo live?'

Flinging her shoes and umbrella behind her, she lurched forward, her feet slipped on the mud as she lurched onto the tarred surface of the pavement. A horn blared, changing tones as it roared past her. Tires screeched on the highway, and an avalanche of water doused her.

She shook away the drenching water as she searched for Kezo. Through the deluge she could see his head and his blue shirt in the churning ditchwater tumbling toward the river's black, roiling whirlpool. A car slid sideways toward her, horn blaring. She spun to the right in a complete circle. In spite of her best efforts, it whacked her leg and burned her fingertips with its hot metal. Heart racing, legs pumping, she sped on toward the deep ditch.

Bracing her feet on the ditch-side, she reached for Kezo. Scrabbling as far as she could reach toward her brother's form in the churning water, her hand only touched his hair as he slipped away from her. Diving into the ditch-full of filthy, waist-high water, she reached for her brother's arm, his hair, his shirt—anything to hold on to. She stretched as far as she could and grabbed at him again. She snagged his shirt collar, pulled him toward her, his weight multiplied against the suck of the current. She stood, drawing the little body closer. A powerful wave slammed into her back. She stumbled, grabbed at a bush—and missed. Again, a gush of water shoved against her. She fell, hitting her head on a boulder edging the ditch and Kezo slipped from her grip.

Staggering forward, her arms at full stretch—she grabbed—with an iron fist she seized his shirt, and with her other hand, she snatched at ditch-side bushes to pull them both to solid ground. Gasping for air, she pounded the back of her limp little brother. He twisted, gagged, then sank into her arms. "Jesus!" she cried. Turning him upside-down, she pounded on his back again and shook him hard.

"Jesus!" She shook Kezo again. Coughing racked her body. "Jesus! Help Kezo!" Blood stained his head and her hands. "Jesus! He's hurt!"

Kezo gagged and his little body convulsed. Again she shook him upside down. Water streamed from his mouth and nose as he vomited. Suddenly, his arms and legs flailed. He gasped in a great breath of air, and then he screamed. Kondi slid to the ground and hugged her little brother to her chest for warmth. Rain continued to pound them both.

Car doors slammed. People shouted. Hands

grasped her arms and lifted her to her feet. Stumbling between two men, she held onto Kezo for dear life. The men thrust her through the doorway of Mai's cookhouse.

Mai screamed and covered her mouth in horror.

Kondi held Kezo out from her body. Terror seized her. Blood covered Kezo's face and her own arms. A buzzing blackness enveloped Kondi. She fell into it and sank to the floor with Kezo still clutched to her chest.

With both her children needing medical help, Mai didn't know which to help first. She fell to the floor by Kondi and Kezo, rocking back and forth and crying, "Jesus! Jesus! Jesus!" Neighbor women slipped between the men standing in the doorway and helped Mai to her feet. They examined Kondi, who was still unconscious on the floor with Kezo's blood all over her head, chest and arms. Another lady tried to comfort Kezo, who continued screaming in terror. He wouldn't stop until they placed him, still coughing and wrapped in a towel, on his mother's lap. Mai clutched her son to her breast and continued to rock back and forth, patting Kezo's back.

"It's not Kezo who's injured; it's Kondi!" one of the women told Mai. She began to cry out, "God, help Kondi, in Jesus' name!"

Bambo Chisale pushed his way through the on-lookers in the crowded doorway. He saw his wife crying with Kezo weeping and coughing on her lap. When he saw Kondi, unconscious on the floor with blood pouring from a ragged cut on her forehead, he fell to his knees, too, and began crying to God to save her. The room seemed filled with shouting, moving people. Some men lifted Bambo to his feet and helped him go outside where he could sit and lean against the wall of the house under the wide eaves.

Inside the house, Mai Chipazi, their neighbor, touched Mai Chisale's arm. "She lives! She lives! She's breathing!" The children's mother stood. Grasping Kezo with one arm and swinging him around behind her, she tied him securely to her back with a *chirundu*. Cuddled next to her warm body and hearing the beat of her heart he would soon fall asleep. Mai knelt beside Kondi on the floor.

"Kondi!" Mai called softly between sobs. "Kondi, my daughter!"

Kondi's eyelids fluttered, and then lay still. Someone pressed a dry cloth to her forehead. Her eyelids lifted slowly, but there was no recognition in her gaze. Suddenly, Kondi shook her head and sat straight up. She coughed, and then swiped at the blood with a trembling hand. "What happened? Where's Kezo?" She looked toward the doorway and scrambled to her feet. "Kezo's in the ditch!" Two of the women clutched her arms to keep her from running outside to find her brother.

"No. He's here!" Mai sobbed and grabbed her

daughter's hand. "You saved his life." Mai turned so Kondi could see Kezo, still sobbing but sleeping peacefully in the *chirundu* sling on his mother's back.

Kondi sank to her knees, wailing in her relief.

Bambo came inside and reached out to touch his children, first rubbing his rough hand over Kezo's head where it rested on his wife's back, and then over Kondi's shuddering shoulders. He patted her over and over again.

Bambo Chipazi, the father of Kondi's next-door friend, Maria, leaned near Bambo's ear. "I will bring my car. You will want to take the children to the hospital, I think."

"*Inde*. Yes. You are very kind." Bambo wiped at his tears.

Mai Chipazi whisked blankets and warm dry clothes for both children from the line hanging from rafter to rafter in the cookhouse. Pushing them into plastic bags, she tied the tops and handed the bags to one of the men to take to the car. Bambo removed his coat and threw it over Kondi's head and shoulders to protect her from the still-pouring rain and keep her warm. When they stepped outside under the wide eaves of the cookhouse, they saw beams of car lights, at odd angles, crisscrossing the paved road with men and policemen moving about between the vehicles.

"I'll tell the policemen they can find you at the hospital," a neighbor murmured to Bambo.

Bambo Chipazi's car drove right into the yard and up to the door of the cookhouse. Other men opened the doors to the car's front and back. When Bambo and Mai Chisale, Kondi and Kezo were inside, men shut the car doors and watched as the car moved away toward the hospital.

In the backseat beside her mother, Kondi rocked back and forth, still clutching the cloth to her injured head. "He's alive!" she whispered over and over. "He's alive."

At the hospital they hurried from the car to the hospital's entrance. Bambo paused to thank Bambo Chipazi for bringing them. "You've blessed us," he said. "*Zikomo*. Thank you."

"I won't return home until I learn what the doctor has to say," Bambo Chipazi said.

Bambo patted his shoulder and followed Mai as she hurried into the building with the children.

🐕 🌲 🐕

The Doctor assured the Chisales that both Kondi and Kezo would be all right, but they must be kept warm. "I'll need to stitch this cut on your daughter's forehead now. Be sure to bring them back if either of them develops a fever or a cough or if you daughter has dizziness or fainting," he said. "I see no reason to keep them in the hospital at this time."

Well after midnight, the Chisale family climbed wearily out of Bambo Chipazi's car in front of their own home. Neighbors covered their mouths with their hands when they saw that Kondi's head was tied with a wide bandage. Bambo thanked Bambo Chipazi, unlocked the door of their house, and led his family inside. When they were ready for bed, Mai Chisale put Kezo in bed with her so she could keep him warmly wrapped. Although the family tossed restlessly for a while, finally peace and sleep descended on their home.

CHAPTER 2

Kondi missed school on Monday. Kezo still coughed a little, but by Tuesday he seemed better. Neither Kondi nor Kezo developed fevers, but Mai continued to hover over them to be sure they were warm and eating well. On Tuesday, Kondi told Mai, "I didn't even feel my head being hit in the ditch, but my head's still throbbing this morning." Mai insisted that she stay home until her headache was gone.

On Wednesday, Kondi didn't tell her mother that her head still pulsed with pain. It would be good to get away from her mother's constant guard. *I know Mai's worrying about us only because she loves us so much, but grown girls like me don't need to be coddled.* She would be glad to be back to school.

That afternoon, before school time, Kondi stopped at Maria's house so they could walk to school together. It seemed like she was always late. Kondi ate a few peanuts while she waited on the path. *If she doesn't come soon, I'll just go on without her.*

Maria finally came out of the house with a textbook balanced on her head and a banana and some peanuts in her hands.

"Did you see the new boy at school yesterday?" Maria asked.

"I didn't go to school yesterday."

"Oh, that's right. You nearly drowned!"

"I didn't nearly drown; but Kezo almost did. At least, we thought he would. I only whacked my head," she touched the white bandage, "and fainted because I was terrified for Kezo. Our whole family was."

"Mmmm, I would have been too. I'm glad you're both all right."

"Mai's still worried about me, of course, so I can't be late coming home this evening. If you're not ready when it's time to leave school . . . "

"I will be," Maria said.

But she wasn't. As Kondi waited at the edge of the playground close to the elephant grass encircling their school playground, she saw Maria talking with a boy, a handsome young man, near one corner of the playground. Who was he, anyway? But she didn't wait any longer and turned toward home.

The same thing happened on Thursday when school let out. Maria and the young man stayed talking near the corner of the school property. "I need to have a talk with Maria," Kondi muttered to herself. "Doesn't she understand it's dangerous to stand chatting with young men when it's growing dark."

The next day, as they walked to school, Maria said, "Max wants to meet you. I told him how bravely you saved your brother from drowning. I've pointed you out to him."

"Who's Max?"

"He's the new boy I was talking to yesterday."

"He's no boy; he's a man. You shouldn't be talking with strange man near the school. He can't be a student, surely."

"He is! He's in Form Four—nearly finished with high school." Maria fussily adjusted the *chirundu* tied around her waist and looked at Kondi from the corner of her eye. "He thinks I'm pretty."

"Of course you're pretty! Anybody can see that. But you need to stay away from grown boys who flatter you, Maria. Don't be silly."

"I'm just listening to him talk, Kondi. There's nothing wrong with talking to a handsome boy."

"He's not a boy—he's a man. Just don't go anywhere with him." Kondi turned and clutched her friend's arm. "He may be attractive to you, but please, stay on the school grounds. You're my friend and I don't want anything bad to happen to you."

"Nothing bad will happen, Kondi. We're just talking."

"I don't like your 'just talking' with a man who stays close to the brush. If he wants to meet me, he needs to come near the school buildings. I won't talk with him otherwise."

When school let out, Kondi found Maria sitting

on a bench by the schoolhouse wall. Max sat beside her. Kondi walked over and Maria introduced them to each other. The three of them chatted for a minute, but Kondi scowled the entire time and gave only short answers when Max asked her questions.

Soon she said, "We need to go home now, Maria. It's dark, and our mothers will need us to help at home." When they walked away Maria looked back at Max.

"What's he want, anyway?" Kondi asked.

"He doesn't want anything except someone to talk to," Maria assured her. "He said both his parents died not long ago—way too early in their lives. He's just lonely and needs someone to visit with."

"I'm not so sure," Kondi said. But why? There seemed to be something 'shifty' about his eyes. He made her feel uneasy. For an orphan boy, he seemed very well fed. And all his clothes looked new. Most school kids had at least a few well-worn clothes.

For several days, the three of them chatted together in the school grounds. Then one Friday Max walked with them along the path through the elephant grass to the road. When they parted not far from the school, Max called to Kondi to come back. "I need to tell you something," he said.

His tone of voice sounded secretive to Kondi, and she glanced around to be sure other people were nearby. Several adults passed by not far away or bought fruit from a roadside vendor, so she relaxed and walked back to him.

"I need you to help me," he said in a low voice.

"You're a big boy–almost a man!" Kondi said in a conversational tone. "Why do you need my help?"

"Shhh. Talk quietly. I need you to help me tomorrow night."

"Sorry. I don't go anywhere at night," Kondi said, turning back toward Maria.

"Please. You're strong and protective." He scuffed the toe of his shoe in the dirt. "And I need your help."

"Well, like I said, I don't go out at night. I stay at home with my parents. Sometimes, early in the evening, I visit Maria and her family, our neighbors. Mai and I sometimes go to their place, if our work's done at home. Otherwise, we stay at our own place after dark."

While they spoke, clouds rolled in. Random drops began to splat on the dry ground making wet circles as big as ten-*tambala* coins.

"You could earn some money." Max's voice wheedled.

"I don't need money." Kondi turned to walk away.

"Wait!" Max called. He reached out and grasped her arm. "I really need your help tomorrow night."

Although there was something very appealing about Max, Kondi felt uneasy and shook his hand off. She walked on. "Sorry," she said. "I need to get home." The rain began to fall in earnest now, and she knew in minutes she would be caught in another torrent.

Max ran after her and grabbed her arm again. He pulled her into the partial shelter of a broad-leafed tree. "You have a little brother, don't you?" His fingers on her arm felt like steel, but the soft, silky tone of his voice made Kondi's blood run cold. Goosebumps raised the hair on her arms.

"Yes," she said, looking him in the eye, "but what's my brother got to do with you?" *Please, God, don't let him hear the fear in my voice!*

"You wouldn't want him to be hurt, now would you?"

Kondi's jaw dropped. His voice made her think of warm oil. In an instant it could become hot enough to burn. A nervous quaking began in her stomach and spread outward until her knees and arms grew weak.

"You leave my brother alone!" Kondi tried to make her voice ring with authority, but to her own ear it sounded pretty weak. She leaned against the tree trunk.

"Oh, yes!" His voice still sounded oily. "I wouldn't think of touching your brother..."

"Good! You'd better not!"

"...if you'll help me tomorrow night."

"I can't! I won't!"

"Oh, yes, you will." Max put his hand in his pocket and took out a large pocketknife. He touched a button on the side, and a sharp silver blade flicked out with a snap. "You will help me. It will only take a few minutes." He ran a finger along the sharp edge of the blade and jerked his hand away, pretending he'd been cut.

Kondi reached her hand out to plead with

him, but when she realized she was trembling she pulled it back. "Please," she said. "Please!"

"I only want you to tell a friend of mine something. It's not a hard thing at all."

"I can't!"

"Yes, you can—and you will. There's nothing wrong with taking a message to my friend, is there?" He plucked a blade of elephant grass. His knife slashed through the air. The end of the grass fell to the ground. "You must help me."

Kondi's knees gave way and she squatted to the ground in horror. She suddenly realized she was soaking wet with rainwater. Pushing herself to her feet and bracing one hand against the tree trunk, she glanced around.

All the nearby adults had found shelter and her school friends had run home. She was all by herself with this monster. She started to run. Max grabbed her arm again. Kondi flinched as though his knife pierced her flesh.

"You will meet me at the crossroads of the M1 and Ncheneka Road at midnight on Saturday. Be there!" His grip on her wrist felt like an iron band and his brown eyes flashed dangerously. "It's not far from your home, so it will be easy for you to meet me there." He waved the knife blade in front of her and then shut it with a snap. "And don't you tell anyone about our conversation or our meeting. Your brother's such a handsome little boy!" Max flung her arm away from his hand and walked away.

Kondi stood under the tree for a minute or

two, breathing hard. When she felt as if she could move without falling, she turned and ran for home.

CHAPTER 3

Kondi sped along until stabs of pain burned in her side and made her slow to a walk. Soon, panic forced her to pick up her pace and kept her trotting toward home, taking great gulps of cool air. Suddenly, lightning flashed. She flinched and covered her face with her hands. When a car honked at her, she jerked her hands away, and found she was standing in the middle of the M1 highway pavement.

Through the heavy rainfall, Kondi could see Mai's cookhouse at the end of the soggy path on the other side of the tarmac. Smoke seeped through the grass roofing and poured over the eaves like a filmy, silk scarf. She staggered across the road, through the ditch, and down their home path. Ducking under the low roofline, she collapsed against the cookhouse wall for a moment before she entered.

"Kondi, you're late!" Mai began to scold. Then she gasped. "And soaking wet. Again!" Mai rose from her low stool by the smoky cooking fire near the center of the room, grabbed a long, dry towel from the line hanging from rafter to rafter, and pushed it toward her daughter.

Kondi shook out the drenched skirt of her school uniform. "I'm sorry, Mai," she said. She slipped off her shoes near the fire and stripped off her sweater and the uniform, throwing them over the line until she could wring them out. Taking the towel, she shuddered, blotting at her dripping braids, rubbing at the goose bumps on her arms, and huddling so close to the fire her underskirt began to steam.

"What happened?" Mai asked. "Why are you so late? It's after dark!"

"Teacher let us out late, Mai, and, of course it's pouring rain." Kondi toweled her face. "And then— uh, someone wanted to talk. In this pouring rain! I thought I'd never get home."

Kondi scrubbed at her wet legs. "I didn't go to Mai Banda's to buy eggs like you asked. I just wanted to come home and, besides, I was sure you'd want me to get dry clothes first and an umbrella." She knew she was chattering like a monkey, but she couldn't help herself. "The *kwacha* you gave me to buy the eggs with is probably soaked."

She picked at the pocket sewn into her soaking half-slip, holding it away from her as she plucked the soggy paper bill from the pocket's corner. *Mai would be horrified if I told her about Max's threats. I can't tell her—not now anyway.*

"I'm sorry, Mai. I'll go get the eggs as soon as the rain stops."

"It's all right, child." Mai took the towel and rubbed the girl's back dry. "Stop babbling. I won't punish you. Kezo can go without an egg until morning. Sit there by the fire, and warm yourself."

While Kondi stepped out of her soaked half-slip and wrapped herself in a dry *chirundu*, Mai took another dry towel from the line and handed it to her daughter. Kondi flung it around her shoulders as Mai pushed her toward the low stool by the fire. "You were right to get out of the storm."

Mai turned toward the teakettle sitting near the fire, a spiral of steam rising from its spout. She lifted the lid and put in some tealeaves. When the tea finished steeping, Mai used the corner of her own *chirundu* to protect her hands, grasped the metal handle and poured tea into a tin cup. She added two spoonsful of sugar, stirred, and handed it to Kondi. "Here, this will warm you up."

Shivering with cold, Kondi took the cup and immediately set it on the floor by her feet so none of the hot liquid would slosh out onto her shaking hands. She snuggled under the thick towel and huddled as close to the fire as she could until her body stopped trembling and her teeth stopped chattering. Then, lifting the cup to her lips, she sipped the tea gratefully.

"Our teacher's nice, Mai. I like her a lot better than Uncle Kakama," Kondi said.

A shadow crossed her mother's countenance.

Oh no! Kondi place her hand on Mai's arm. "I'm sorry, Mai. I should have liked Uncle Kakama because he's your brother. He was a good teacher but only because we all feared him. This teacher likes us, and we like her too, so we want to learn."

Mai nodded. "I understand, Kondi. There's a big difference. Learning because you love someone is better than learning through fear." Mai pulled up another stool from the corner. "We must continue to pray for my brother. He's heard about God's ways and rejected them, so we can only pray." Mai sat down on the stool and stirred the chicken, onion and tomatoes stewing in the pot.

"Mmm, the *ndiwo* smells good, Mai," Kondi said. "Are guests coming?"

"No, your father gave me extra money to buy food, and I thought it would be nice to have chicken for a change."

Kondi smiled although her muscles still felt shaky with the cold. And with fear.

"I think we will eat dinner a bit early this evening," Mai said. "You need something hot inside you." She stood. "Kezo, no!" She took his hand out of a bag of shelled peanuts and swung him by his arm onto her back, tying him there with an extra *chirundu* she snatched from the line. "I'll make the *nsima* right away."

Setting the stew pot aside, she put the *nthali*, a straight-sided clay pot used to cook porridge, on the three stones of their cooking fire and poured water into it. She did not add rock salt because the *ndiwo* was always plenty salty. When she pushed the burning sticks together more firmly under the pot the fire blazed up. Soon the hot maize porridge would be ready and they could eat.

"Kondi, run to the house and change into dry clothes. Then tell your father I will bring his supper early tonight. Here, take my umbrella."

"Thank you for the tea, Mai. I'm nice and warm now." She pulled the chirundu more tightly around her waist and folded it under twice to keep it snug. Pulling the towel more closely around her shoulders, she pointed Mai's huge red umbrella through the doorway, and opened it outside under the eaves. "I'll go dress in dry clothes and be back in a minute."

As she dashed across the yard to the two-room house where she, her brother, and her parents slept, she remembered a kitchen she seen when visiting a friend in Dedza town. Cooking on a shiny, white stove right inside the house! Imagine the luxury! But since they cooked with an open fire, they would have to use a separate cookhouse so they wouldn't accidentally burn up everything they owned if their fire should get away from them. Maybe, someday, Mai could have a lovely indoor kitchen.

After Kondi ducked under the eaves of the main house and snapped the umbrella shut, she stepped inside and paused in the doorway of the sitting room. Hearing a sound, she looked behind her. Beside the road, a small, ragged, forlorn beggar boy huddled near the trunk of a dense tree. *He looks as wet and cold as I was! I'll tell him to come with me to the cookhouse when I return. He's probably hungry, too.*

23

She glanced toward Bambo's workshop. A light gleamed in the workshop window. Bambo was probably working at his painting. Ukhale, the Chisales' watchdog, dozed under the overhang of the roof.

How strange that Ukhale would let that orphan boy stay in their *bwalo*. He usually barked at even the neighbors who came and went all the time.

Kondi went into the bedroom and slipped into a dry half-slip, a blouse and warm sweater and skirt. Outside, the wind calmed, and the whipping rain settled into a steady downpour. When she went out the door again, the beggar boy had disappeared.

Under the umbrella, she crossed the yard to Bambo's workshop. Through the small window she could see Bambo at the table with a small box in front of him. The lid lay back on the table and Bambo was putting something into it.

On the workshop porch, Kondi stopped long enough to snap the umbrella shut and shake it a couple of times. Then she propped the closed umbrella near the door and twisted the doorknob. The door wouldn't open.

"I'm coming!" Bambo called.

Kondi heard a chair scrape, a rustling sound, and a cupboard close. When Bambo opened the door, she glanced toward the table, but the box was no longer there.

"Mai says we'll have supper early." Kondi smiled. "I got wet coming home from school, and now she's worried because I was so cold. We'll bring your supper to the sitting room in a few minutes." Kondi looked forward to eating in the kitchen, as usual, with Mai and Kezo where it was warm and cozy.

Bambo smiled at Kondi, but his smile didn't quite reach his eyes.

He looked worried. What could be troubling him now? Kondi stepped back onto the porch and closed the door behind her. His paintings were selling well, so she didn't think it would be money worries. Why had he hidden the box when she came to the door? *Oh dear, I don't like secrets.*

She returned across the yard under the red umbrella's protection and found Mai, with Kezo still tied to her back, stooping beside the *nthali* to give the last stir to the thick porridge. Mai put the hefty stirring paddle aside and scooped the thick porridge into patties with a big flat wooden spoon. Dipping it in water between each scoop, she layered the patties of porridge onto a plate and covered the plate with a bowl. She poured the chicken stew into another bowl and covered it, too. Then she set the *nsima* plate and stew dish on a tray and covered the loaded tray with a cloth.

"Here, Mai, let me carry it across to the sitting room."

"I think we will both need to go," Mai said with a smile. "One of us needs to carry the tray and the other the umbrella." Kezo had fallen asleep on Mai's back, although, at three, he was almost too big to be carried anymore.

When Kondi and her mother stepped up onto the

porch of the main house and entered the sitting room, Bambo stood by the table. The kerosene pressure lamp he'd been using in the workshop now hung from the main beam of the house on a hook, filling the room with light. Mai brought a basin of water and a bar of soap to Bambo as Kondi set the tray on the table and uncovered the *nsima* and stewed chicken. A gush of steam swirled up from the food into the cool room. Bambo flicked water from his hands, peered into the bowls of food and pulled back a chair, ready to sit down to his meal.

He stopped. "Why don't you both eat with me tonight?"

Kondi looked at her mother with round eyes. Most fathers she knew never ate with their families. "But we've left our food in the pots in the kitchen, Bambo."

"I'm sure there's enough here for all three of us," he said. "Besides, I'm tired of eating alone. Kezo is asleep, so he can eat what's in the pots when he wakes up."

Mai looked pleased. She nodded and went into the bedroom to lay Kezo down. Kondi pulled two more chairs up to the table. Mai and Kondi sat and waited for Bambo to take the first food from the dishes that all three of them would eat from.

Bambo cleared his throat. "Let's pray."

Kondi's mouth fell open. She glanced at her mother. Bambo never offered to pray over their food. He'd given his heart to Jesus Christ a couple of years before, but he'd never prayed over a meal, even though they knew he loved the Lord. Realizing her mouth hung open, she snapped it shut.

"Father, thank you for this food, and thank you for Mai, who has worked hard to make it taste so good to us. We praise you for all your blessings and your supply for all our needs. Amen."

Kondi had barely the time to fold her hands and bow her head. Did Bambo put extra emphasis on the word "all" in his prayer? She peeked at her mother between her fingers. Mai's face beamed with a great gladness.

CHAPTER 4

On Saturday morning, Kondi rose early. The air caressed her skin with moisture from the previous day's rain, and the ground, though not soggy, felt soft underfoot. The sun, just chinning itself on the eastern hills, made diamonds out of the raindrops glistening on the tall elephant grasses and tree leaves. Kondi shivered, tied her *chirundu* more closely around her waist and ducked back in the house for a second one to cover her shoulders.

As she did every morning, Kondi put the pole on its resting place close to the henhouse door and lowered the other end to the ground. Then she raised the door-hatch to let the chickens out. As they tiptoed down the pole, she stood back and listened to the special clucking of the hens' delight in being set free. When the rooster pushed his head out of the henhouse, he flapped his wings importantly and crowed, "Kokoliko!"

When Kondi started across the *bwalo* toward the

kitchen house, Ukhale bounded up and wagged a friendly good morning. But, something more than this morning's chill was making her feel shivery. What was it? Suddenly she remembered and stopped short. Tonight! What would she do about meeting Max tonight?

Kondi turned toward the highway. Shadows moved at the base of the tree where she'd seen the beggar boy the night before. This morning he'd settled in a spot where the rising sun would warm his back and he'd clasped a thin, ragged blanket around his shoulders. But Kondi could see neither did much to stop his shivering in the chilly air. Poor boy! Her heart ached for him. She would take him a cup of tea when she'd boiled the water.

Kondi walked to the cookhouse, plucked firewood and kindling from the stack behind it and pulled out some dry grass from the underside of its roof. Bambo had told her not to do this, but at the backside of the cookhouse she felt sure it wouldn't be noticed. She built a small fire between the blackened stones and balanced the filled teakettle on them to heat.

When Kondi saw her mother crossing the *bwalo*, she called out a morning greeting. "*Moni*, Mai."

Mai poured water into the basin on the bench by the cookhouse door, splashed some on her face and swiped it dry with the hem of her *chirundu*. "Moni'tu," Mai murmured sleepily. Mai always had a hard time waking up in the morning.

"I have the teakettle on already," Kondi said. "May I give the beggar boy some tea when it's ready?"

"Mmm." Mai nodded and disappeared into the cookhouse.

"I'll go down to Mai Banda's and get the eggs I couldn't get last night," Kondi called after her mother. "Kezo needs an egg for his breakfast."

The sun poured warmth over the back of the shivering beggar boy and beamed a bright ray of orange light across a huge gray cloud hovering over Dedza Mountain. As Kondi walked near him, she paused to say, "I'll bring you some tea and bread when I return from the egg farm." He nodded his head slowly but he didn't reply. A deep cough shook his body.

When she reached the chicken farm she approached the door of Mrs. Banda's cookhouse and coughed loudly. "*Hodi*," she called. "May I come in?"

"*Lowani!*" Mai Banda called back. "Enter!"

Kondi ducked her head to go through the low doorway. Mai Banda was just steeping tea for her own family.

"I've come to buy eggs, Mai. Am I too early?"

"*Iai*. No, you're not. I'll get them for you in just a minute."

Kondi explained about getting home late from school the night before, and how the rainstorm kept her from coming then for the eggs. "But Kezo needs an egg for his breakfast, so I'm early this morning."

"You are kind to your baby brother."

"He's a special gift from God to our family. You may remember that when he was born we weren't sure he'd would live—nor Mai either—so we appreciate both of them a lot."

"Mmm." Mai Banda nodded her head. "Yes, I heard." Mai Banda set the teakettle filled with brewing tea near the fire to keep warm until her family was ready for breakfast. "How many eggs do you want?"

"Three would be enough."

"Just three? The sale of three eggs will not feed my family today."

Kondi hid a smile. Mai Banda used many cunning ways to pressure her customers into buying more eggs than they really wanted.

After paying, Kondi started home with the eggs tied into a plastic sack. She looked south toward the spot where the pavement met the dirt track to Ncheneka, their old home. Fear clenched her throat as she thought again of Max and his threats.

However, the person she could see in the distance crossing from the village lane toward Dedza town was not Max. It looked like Ulemu Mbewe, the pastor's daughter and her dearest friend from Ncheneka Village, their old home. It had been hard for Kondi to leave Ulemu behind when they'd moved closer to town, where Bambo could more easily sell his paintings.

It is Ulemu! I recognize her!

"Mimi!" Kondi shouted Ulemu's nickname. She waved wildly, forgetting about the eggs.

When the person glanced in her direction, Kondi waved frantically with her free hand. Perhaps Ulemu couldn't see her well in the early morning light. "Ulemu! I am your best friend, Kondi!" It had to be Ulemu. She remembered the blue dress she was wearing. It *was* Ulemu.

Ulemu started to wave, stopped, put her hand to her mouth, and then dashed away across the thoroughfare toward town.

Now why would Ulemu not wait to talk to her? They'd been best friends for years, since they were just toddlers. Their parents had lived close to each other in Ncheneka Village until the Chisale family moved away. She used to see Ulemu every day–even at church.

Kondi trudged home with her head down. Why had she run away without even saying hello? That wasn't even polite. Mai Chisale had taught Kondi that it was simply polite to stop and greet friends one met on the way to or from town—even when in a big hurry. Surely, Ulemu's mother taught her to do the same.

A few minutes later, she entered their cookhouse to put the three eggs in an enamel dish on the shelf where Mai would find them. She walked across the *bwalo* near the porch of the main house and called, "Mai! I'm going to town. I saw Ulemu and I want to talk to her. I won't be long. I promised the beggar boy some tea and bread. Would you give it to him, please?"

"*Inde*," Mai called from inside the house.

Kondi took a banana from the stalk hanging under the eaves of the cookhouse and put it on her head while she used both hands to wrap her *chirundu* more tightly around her waist. Then she started off, taking the banana from its resting place and peeling it as she walked along.

When she rounded the corner of the path by Maria's house, she found Maria just heading for town too. "Let's walk together," Maria said. Kondi really wanted to go alone because she wanted time to think. Why had Ulemu ignored her? She'd never done such a thing before. But Kondi nodded and she and Maria started along the path together.

Maria chattered away and didn't seem to notice how quiet Kondi was when they neared the crossroads.

This is the very place where I'll need to meet Max if I want him not to hurt Kezo. Maybe I should just tell Bambo about what Max said and let Bambo take care of it. Kondi hurried Maria on toward town. *But what if Bambo couldn't stop Max from hurting Kezo!* Kondi's blood ran like icy water into her fingertips.

Soon the two girls passed the rows of police housing, the school, and the old post office. The market was just ahead.

"I'm going in here, Maria. I'll see you later."

"Oh, I'm going to the market, too," Maria said.

Kondi sighed. She really wanted to see Ulemu

alone, and she was pretty sure Ulemu was already inside. "All right. But I may find my friend inside and I need to talk to her about something. Alone."

They stopped at the gate to show their identification indicating they'd paid their income tax.

"Ahhh, here's the girl who gives me trouble every time she comes," the gateman muttered. "I wonder what trouble you will cause today."

Kondi shifted her feet uncomfortably, remembering how rude she'd been to this gateman on the day Kezo was born and Mai was so sick in the hospital. She felt the heat of embarrassment creep up her neck.

When the gateman waved them through with his boney hand, Kondi glanced about, searching the customers to find Ulemu.

The racket at the tinsmiths' stalls nearly gave her a headache, so she put her fingers in her ears as she walked by. She stepped over homemade rope and long strips of old tire inner tubing people used for tying their bundles onto bicycles or to car roof racks. Kondi looked here and there as she passed the housewares stall with its display of enamel dishes, cups, pots, pans and teakettles. Surely, Ulemu would be found in the market somewhere.

Next, Kondi headed for the sheds where vegetables and fruits stood in heaps on clean cloths. Stacks of cabbages, piles of tomatoes and hot green peppers, and heaps of dried beans and rice made colorful mounds on tables under the shed roof.

Another aisle displayed papayas, oranges, tangerines, mangoes, lemons, and pineapples with their prickly tops pointed upward.

She saw a familiar blue dress whisk out of sight behind a display of clothes hanging from a rafter. It was the dress she'd seen Ulemu wear many times. Kondi hurried to the spot as fast as she could dart between customers. But Ulemu wasn't behind the dresses. Kondi was just in time to see a flash of blue going out the market gateway in the distance.

Tears blurred Kondi's vision. *Ulemu saw me waving at her so she knows it's me. Why doesn't she want to talk to me?*

Kondi went back to find Maria. "I'm ready to go home," she said. It was nearly mid-morning, but Maria needed to go on to the post office, so Kondi started back towards home alone.

Every time she walked around the corner of a building or turned a bend, Kondi looked ahead hoping to see Ulemu or even a glimpse of her blue dress. When Kondi came to the long straight stretch of road near the police houses, she could see someone in blue crossing the pavement in the distance, but the person was too far away for Kondi to identify. *I wanted to talk to Ulemu and find out all the news from home.*

When she finally reached their *bwalo* and saw the familiar figure of her mother coming out of the cookhouse she almost started to cry. Missing a chat with Ulemu had been bad enough. Now what was she going to do about meeting Max at midnight? She wished she could ask Mai, but Max said she couldn't tell anyone, or....

"Kondi, what's wrong?" Mai asked.

"I'm not sure if anything's wrong or not, Mai. I thought I saw Ulemu crossing toward Dedza, but now I'm not sure. I waved, but she wouldn't stop and talk to me."

"That doesn't sound like Ulemu," Mai replied. "She's always friendly and chatty--since you both were toddlers."

"I know. Now I'm not sure. But, whoever it was, wore a blue dress just like Ulemu's and now I really miss her."

"I understand, Kondi. Why don't we go to the Ncheneka Village church tomorrow morning, instead of the town church? Then you could see Ulemu and talk with her."

Kondi's face brightened. "Going there would be really nice, Mai."

"I'll talk with Bambo about it. He may want to come with us. Now stop worrying and go turn the clothes on the line. I washed them alone this morning while you went to town." Like most housewives in Malawi, Mai just draped the freshly washed clothes over the clothesline. Clothespins were a luxury they couldn't afford.

When Kondi dropped the fifth garment, she went to wash and rinse it again. Then she began turning the rest. She dropped another one.

"Kondi, you'll never finish if you have to keep rinsing the clothes you drop. Don't be so careless!"

Mai scolded from the cookhouse doorway.

"Sorry, Mai." Kondi's hands shook as she glanced again at the sun, lowering itself toward the horizon inch by inch. *What am I going to do? I just won't go, that's all. Max wouldn't hurt Kezo. Or would he?*

Another garment flopped to the ground out of her shaking hand. She snatched it up quickly. She hoped Mai didn't see.

"You're wasting water, Kondi! And soap."

I should have known she'd notice.

When Mai asked her to make the *nsima* for supper, she spilled *ufa* on the dirt floor of the cookhouse. After they finished their supper, she nearly dropped the *nthali* when she started to wash it.

"What's wrong with you, Kondi? All day, you've been dropping things!" Mai's frown showed her puzzlement. "You aren't usually careless."

I wish I could tell Mai what's making me so nervous and afraid. But I can't. Max would hurt Kezo. I keep telling myself he wouldn't, but I know he would.

"I'm just tired, Mai." She didn't want to worry Mai and Bambo with her problems. But Max threatened to.... "I think I'll go to bed early tonight."

However, once she was on her mat and covered with her blanket, she couldn't sleep. Her thoughts darted to one possibility and another. *I have to meet Max. I can't let anything happen to Kezo.*

CHAPTER 5

In the bedroom of the main house, Kondi picked up the small kerosene lamp Bambo made from a lidded jar and opened it to add some kerosene. Using a hammer and a nail, Bambo had punched a hole in the lid and then he'd pulled a bit of twisted rag through the hole. Once the lid was screwed on, Kondi lit a match and touched it to the wick. The rag sucked up the kerosene in the jar fueling the flame above the lid. The lamp couldn't be used for long, since the rag burned up, too, but it gave enough light for her to get ready for bed.

She flung her school uniform over the wire strung across a corner of the room and wrapped her other dirty clothes in a bundle to put near the doorway where she could easily find it in the morning and take outside to wash. Unrolling her mat in a corner of the living room, she licked her fingers and pinched out the wick, wrapped her blanket securely around herself, and lay down on her mat.

She could hear Kezo's soft breathing in the

bedroom where, an hour ago, Mai had lain him to sleep. For a few minutes she stared at the pale square of moonlit sky showing through the door window. A moth fluttered at the glass, its shadow, danced in a square of moonlight on the floor of the pitch-dark room. When she became sleepy she covered her head to keep mosquitoes from biting her. Even then, she couldn't sleep.

After what seemed like a long time, Mai came in to prepare for bed, too. Presently, Kondi heard the bed frame squeak as Mai climbed into bed and settled herself next to Kezo.

Soon the door rattled softly again. Kondi's eyes flew open. Through a thin spot in her blanket, she could see a gleam of lamplight. *Pretend to be asleep. If you* do *decide to meet Max at the crossroads, you don't want Bambo to know you were even awake.*

Bambo came in with his lantern set very low. He moved quietly as he closed the door and twisted the key in the lock. He cleared his throat softly and she heard him step near to check on his sleeping daughter. *Breathe deeply!* It felt like lying, but she was supposed to be asleep.

Kondi felt Bambo spread another blanket over her against the chilly night. *Thank you, God. I know Bambo loves me.* A flush of embarrassment warmed her cheeks. *Please forgive me for deceiving him.*

After a few minutes, through the bedroom doorway, she heard the bed frame creak when Bambo, too, climbed into bed.

Kondi pulled back the edge of the blanket. A

cloud covering the moon made the pale square at the window dim. *How will I know when it's midnight?* Her heart raced with fear and her breath came in gasps. *I don't need to know. I won't go!* She turned over and covered her face again.

What will Max do to Kezo if I don't go? Her breath caught and her heart suddenly felt like a rock. She could feel the goose bumps creep along her chest, down her arms, and up her neck. *This is silly! Surely Max wouldn't really hurt Kezo, would he?*

She rubbed her arms under the blanket and shifted. She kept assuring herself that he wouldn't hurt her baby brother. He wouldn't! No decent person could. But then she remembered Max's hands pulling the knife from his pocket, the *s-s-snick* of the flashing blade, his jerk as he pretended to cut his finger. He'd held the knife in front of her as his silken voice, filled with menace, implied what he would do to hurt Kezo.

Lord, have mercy! He would! I know he would. She threw the blankets back and tiptoed into her parents' bedroom. Quietly, she took the clock from the top of the chest of drawers and crept back into the living room. Eleven-fifteen. There was still time to decide. She put the clock on the edge of the table where she could just see its iridescent dial in the dark. Quietly, she went back into her parents' bedroom, felt for her clothes and a sweater, took them into the living room and laid them over a chair by the table.

Sitting back on her mat, she wrapped her blankets closely around her. Then, lying down on her side, she watched the clock, and again went over the pros and cons for doing what Max ordered. Neither option seemed right.

The glowing minute hand crept around the dial more slowly than she thought possible. As she stared at it, she changed her mind a dozen times about whether to meet Max or stay safe at home. *But I have to keep Kezo safe!* At ten minutes to twelve, she tossed her blanket back and sat up.

You're being a foolish girl! She put on her clothes and threw a thick sweater around her shoulders. *The last time you wandered around in the middle of the night, you ended up running for your life and knocked yourself out when you fell and hit your head on a boulder!* She picked up her shoes and carefully unlocked the door. She held her breath when the key clicked in the lock and winced when the door squeaked on its hinges. No one stirred.

She stepped outside and eased the door closed behind her. Ukhale thumped his tail at this unexpected meeting with Kondi under the eaves. Stopping in the white moonlight to put on her shoes, she headed down the path to where M1 and Ncheneka Road met a few yards away. She sat on the large, flat stone in the deep darkness beneath the huge mango tree.

If he wasn't so good looking, would I be meeting him here? She puffed out a breath of disgust at herself. *Besides, I'm not really meeting him. He's not going to see me.*

Nothing moved except the shifting shadows of

the shrubs and trees at the edge of the track. Kondi shifted on her hard stone in the mango tree's deep moon-shade and waited. The wind hissed through the elephant grass and the tree leaves rattled above her. After what seemed like a long time, she entered the elephant grass and crept through to the edge of the intersection. She checked each way along the highway and peered down Ncheneka Road. Only a cat crept from the elephant grass on a mouse hunt.

She had returned to her stone seat when she suddenly felt a tickle in the back of her nose. *Oh no! I can't sneeze now!* The tickle kept on building. She scrubbed her nose this way and that. *I can't stop it!* She grabbed her nostrils closed and clamped her mouth against the eruption. P-p-p-p! Only a tiny sound came out. Kondi looked around. Had anyone heard her?

As far as she could see, nothing out of the ordinary moved. Clouds scudded across the sky, covering and uncovering the moon. Only the cat dashed away across the road and into the ditch on the other side.

There! I didn't see anyone! And more importantly, nobody saw me!

An owl hooted in a nearby tree and she heard the rush of its wings as it swooped low over their *bwalo* and disappeared into the darkness. Kondi shivered. Everyone knew an owl was an meant something bad was going to happen. She settled back onto her sitting-stone under the mango tree. *Silly!* There was no such thing as bad luck—at least not the kind brought on by an owl hooting.

The moon dipped behind Dedza Mountain, throwing the nearby ground into deeper darkness. *Go home, you foolish girl. God is in control of your life—and Kezo's. You need to trust Him.* She stood and started for home, only to stumble over a root and fall. Impatiently, she stood and brushed the twigs and grass from her knees, dusted her hands, and checked for scrapes.

When she slipped across their *bwalo* at home, she eased the door open and shut, locking it behind her. Undressing, she covered herself on her mat and instantly fell into a deep sleep.

"Kondi!"

Kondi uncovered her head and raised it. "Hmm?"

"It's time to get up. We have to leave at sunrise if we're going to Ncheneka Village church."

Kondi groaned. It seemed like only minutes since she'd come back to bed. However, she threw back her blankets and stood as eagerly as she could. It would be so nice to see all their old friends at their church back in the village, especially Ulemu.

"That's strange!" Mai stopped beside Kondi's mat and stared at the clock on the table. "How did the clock get in here?" Mai asked.

Kondi felt a cold chill rush up her back. Her hand went to her mouth.

"I thought sure the clock was on the chest of drawers when I climbed into bed last night."

Kondi's shivered. "Could Bambo have moved it?" Her voice sounded shaky even to herself.

She grabbed her clothes, yanked them over her head and rushed outside behind the house. She leaned against the wall until her hands stopped shaking, and then stepped out to put up the pole to the chicken house and let the hens and rooster out of their high coop. Ukhale moved from his sleeping place beside their corn storehouse and slowly wagged his tail.

After a few minutes, Mai called from the cookhouse. "Kondi, I have tea ready,"

Thank you God! She didn't ask me if I'd moved the clock!

In order to arrive on time at the church in Ncheneka Village, the Chisales needed to leave their house at daybreak for the six-mile walk. Thinking about seeing Ulemu made the journey pass more quickly for Kondi. By the time Kondi and her family neared the church and entered the door, joyful singing filled the air. Mai and Kondi, with Kezo sleeping on her back, sat with women and girls on the right side of the church. Bambo joined the men and boys on the other. Toddlers and young children sat on a mat placed on the floor at the front of the church where their parents and church ushers could keep an eye on them.

From the back of the church, Kondi saw Ulemu sitting a few rows down and purposely moved to sit beside her friend. Ulemu glanced at her and scooted over to make room, but she gave no welcoming smile. She just nervously licked of her lips and looked out the window.

What was wrong with Ulemu? Didn't she even want to be friends with Kondi anymore? Kondi settled into her place and tucked her *chirundu* more securely around her knees. She bowed her head for a short prayer while the rest of the congregation finished their hymn. When her prayer was finished, she looked at Ulemu and smiled, but Ulemu didn't smile in return, although Kondi thought she saw a friendlier gleam in Ulemu's expression.

"We want to welcome our guests today," Pastor Mbewe announced in his fine voice. "We're especially glad to have the Chisale family with us this morning." Pastor Mbewe's friendly smile beamed his pleasure. "Welcome back to your home church. Please enter into the worship of God with us wholeheartedly."

People turned in their seats to smile at the Chisale family. Some women nearby shook hands with Mai. Many in the congregation nodded. Men welcomed Bambo.

A feeling of comfort, of coming home, filled Kondi's heart until she noticed again how uncomfortable Ulemu was, shifting on the bench beside her, gazing at the floor and folding a corner of her *chirundu* first one way, then another.

For the rest of the service Kondi worried about what was wrong with Ulemu. She didn't hear even one word of Pastor Mbewe's sermon. As everyone stood to sing the closing hymn, Kondi reached over and put her arm through Ulemu's like she'd done for years. After a bit Ulemu gently pulled away. Kondi sighed in distress.

As the final amen was said, Kondi reached for Ulemu's hand, but Boniko, a girl from the village known for her sassy ways, grabbed Kondi's shoulders and spun her around toward the aisle.

"It's so nice to see you back home where you belong!" Boniko said. But something in her voice made it sound like a mockery. Boniko came to church all the time, but it didn't seem to help change her life or her ways.

She talked politely with Boniko for a minute and then turned to say something to Ulemu. But Ulemu was gone. Kondi craned her neck to search every corner of the room. She wasn't even in the building!

Mai Mbewe invited the Chisale family to eat at their house before they walked home and Kondi's heart leaped. She'd be able to chat with Ulemu at her own home. Surely she'd be willing to talk with her there!

But Ulemu wasn't around when the Chisales arrived. As Mai Mbewe served their food, Kondi said, "I was hoping to be able to visit with Ulemu. Is she here?"

A sad and worried expression flooded Mai Mbewe's face. "She's not been herself lately." She glanced around. "I don't know where she's gone."

When it was time for the Chisales to start for home, Kondi said to Mai Mbewe, "Please tell Ulemu I miss her and I said goodbye."

Bambo strode ahead with Kezo on his shoulders. After they'd walked a ways, Mai asked, "Kondi, did you get a chance to talk with Ulemu at church?"

"No, I didn't." Kondi fingers fiddled with a leaf she'd picked from a nearby bush. "She disappeared. I don't know where she went."

"I noticed she wasn't there at lunch to help her mother serve food, either," Mai said. "That's unusual. Ulemu's always been a great help to her mother."

"What could be wrong with her, Mai? I don't want her to be sad and worried."

"I know you don't. I don't either. But sometimes girls have upsets in their friendships. I'm sure it will work itself out in time. Besides, she'll walk into town for school tomorrow, so you'll see her then."

Kondi nodded, bit her lip, and gazed soberly at the far, blue mountains as they walked along. "Yes, I hope I will," she said. But her heart still felt heavy and sad.

CHAPTER 6

When Kondi arrived at school at twenty minutes past three on Monday afternoon, she paused where the school path opened into the playground. She tightened the *chirundu* she wore over her school uniform as she looked all around the school grounds for Ulemu. Finally, she saw her standing under a tree at the edge of the playing field.

What was Ulemu doing leaning forward and talking to a man? She wasn't really chatty with very many people—certainly not a stranger.

The next moment, Ulemu straightened and disappeared around the back of the school. Who could that man be? Maria moved up to talk with him and Kondi sharpened her gaze.

"Oh my goodness, it's Max!" Kondi whispered to herself. "He looks like a man with his hair slicked back, and he's big enough to be a man. Ulemu may not be chatty, but Max could talk the leg off a donkey. And now silly Maria is. What a fool I was last Friday to be afraid of what he said."

He *was* good-looking, though. Kondi remembered how his even teeth gleamed white, making his smile dimple on one side. The thought made her heart catch. Her eyes widened at the memory of the ripple of light along his muscles when he flexed his arm. Her initial feeling of wariness had been replaced with an attraction that made her heart beat faster. He was older than the rest of the boys at school, but that wasn't so unusual. Many boys had to work to support their families. It could be many years, for some of them, before they finished their schooling.

Kondi looked all over the school grounds for Ulemu, but she didn't find her until class began. Instead of sitting next to Kondi, Ulemu chose a desk on the far side of the room.

At their meal break, Kondi headed toward Ulemu before she could go out of their schoolroom. "Hi, Mimi!" she said, using the affectionate nickname she'd used for her since they were small children. "Let's eat together, okay?" Kondi hooked her arm through her friend's, and they moved off together with their snacks. When they emerged from the building, Ulemu hung back, but Kondi urged her on.

Kondi found a shady spot under the eaves, and they sat on a small projection of the building's foundation stones with their feet in the rain gutter. They didn't have to worry about getting their feet wet today with the sun setting in the west. They each bowed their heads to thank God silently for their food.

"Now, what's wrong?" Kondi asked as she knuckled kernels off her roasted cob of corn.

Ulemu focused her gaze on a small stick in the ditch. She shoved it around with her shoe and cleared her throat. No words seemed to come so she just shook her head.

"Something's wrong between us, so don't try to say there isn't." Kondi offered her some corn kernels. "What have I done to hurt your feelings?"

"Nothing," Ulemu whispered, picking three corn kernels from Kondi's hand. She kept pushing at the stick with her toe. She cleared her throat again. "You've done nothing wrong," she said. With her thumb she fumbled the corn kernels around in her palm.

"Then why are you avoiding me?" Kondi refused to leave their situation unresolved. "You know you have been."

Ulemu lowered her head in embarrassment and nodded her head. "But it's not you, Kondi. It's me. I just seem to want to be alone now for some reason."

Kondi noticed her expression, indicating Ulemu knew the reason very well. "What is it? You know you can tell me anything, and you'll still be my best friend—just like we have been since we were tiny."

"I know I would." Tears pooled in the corners of Ulemu's eyes. "But I have to decide something for myself."

Kondi gave an exasperated sigh. "Sometimes two people can figure things out better than only one,

Ulemu."

"I know, but I just can't tell you right now!" Ulemu stood, tossed the corn kernels in the ditch, grabbed her *chirundu* more closely around her and dashed around the corner of the school building.

Now tears pooled in the corners of Kondi's eyes, too. "I wish she'd just *tell* me and get it over with!" she murmured. "Please, God, help Ulemu to do what's right and to speak the truth. And help her sort out what's bothering her."

She heard a small sound. Max stood in front of her, propped on one leg with the other braced against the edge of the ditch while he twisted some stalks of dry grass back and forth in his hands.

"Ulemu seems upset," he said, giving her a lazy smile. Max had moved so quietly she'd barely heard him—only his closest footsteps. A grass stem bobbed in the corner of his mouth when he spoke and the dimple in his cheek came and went. "Did she tell you anything?" His dimple came and went as he smiled.

Kondi's heart seemed to turn over in her chest, a new, strange but delightful sensation. "We talked, but she didn't say much. She'll be all right, though," she said. "I just prayed for her." So why was she feeling happy when her best friend was in such distress?

"Oh, prayer doesn't work. I've tried it!" He shifted from one foot to the other. "My mother prayed, but it doesn't work for me." Sunlight rippled across his curly hair and gleamed over his cheekbones.

"It's not a matter of making prayer work for you.

Prayer is making a connection with God. You can ask for things, believing He will answer and you can submit to His will, knowing He's all powerful and good. He'll give you what He knows you need."

"Hmmm. Are you a philosopher or a woman preacher?"

"Neither. I'm just a girl who loves God. I know He loves me, too."

"Well, I'm such a bad boy I guess I'd better leave."

"Silly. If you know you're a bad boy, why avoid those who love God? Avoiding godly people won't change anything. Just tell God you're sorry for your past and ask Him to help you change your ways."

"Well, He wouldn't love me." Max's glance dropped to the ground and then darted away to the horizon. "I know He wouldn't!"

Kondi cleared her throat and stood, brushing bread and corncob crumbs from her skirt. "That's not true." She shook her head. "In the Bible God says He loves you. He loves you so much He sent His Only Son to die for you, Max." She pointed her finger at him for emphasis. "If you accept Christ's sacrifice for you, you won't have to feel guilty or ashamed."

"I'm glad you're happy. The god I serve is angry with me all the time. I have to give him things and make sacrifices to keep him happy. Then I can feel free."

"Well, you'll only know true happiness when you accept Christ as your Savior. Jesus said, 'I am the way, the truth, and the life. No one comes to God except through me.'"

The school bell rang. Across the school grounds, students scurried to their classrooms.

"So why did you go to the crossroad last Saturday at midnight then? Because you trust Him so much?" Max started to walk away.

Suddenly, she went cold all over, and clapped both hands to her mouth. "You were there?" Shame flooded her heart.

"Yes, but not the whole time." Max's glance flicked over her face and a derisive smile played around his mouth. "I didn't see you until you sneezed. You were still there when I started home."

"But I didn't meet you!" Kondi shivered now.

"Oh, you were there all right." His voice was silken now. "Stumbling and falling wasn't such a good thing to do, either."

He was *there!* Kondi's heart raced and then stopped with a thud. "I only looked. I didn't obey you. I didn't do what you ordered."

Max grinned broadly. The grass stem in his mouth bobbed merrily up and down.

Kondi felt as if she'd turned to stone. She couldn't even stand as she stared at him.

"But you will," Max whispered. "Yes, you will! Meanwhile, watch out for your little brother." He began to whistle as he sauntered away.

When Kondi came home from school, she

carefully put her books away in the sitting room before she went to the cookhouse where her mother was making supper. "Mai, I talked with Ulemu at school. She wouldn't tell me what's wrong." She plunked down on a low stool beside the fire stretching her hands toward its warmth. "She sat close to the door this afternoon and left as soon as the class dismissed."

"I think you should stop worrying about this, Kondi." Mai pulled her own stool closer to give the *ndiwo* another stir. "You've been best friends since you were babies. This small upset isn't going to ruin a lifelong friendship. It will sort itself out in time."

"It's the time I don't like, Mai. I want it sorted out now!"

"I know." Mai looked up from her stirring to give Kondi a smile. "You youngsters always hurry. Adults more willingly wait for time to take its course."

"I can't think of a thing I've done to offend her."

"You probably haven't, my daughter. It will come right before long. Meanwhile, have you prayed about it or prayed for Ulemu?"

Kondi felt the blood rush into her cheeks. "Yes, I have." She stood and adjusted her *chirundu*. "But not as often as I should. I'll go and pray for her again." She put her hand on Mai's shoulder. "Thank you for being such a good mother and reminding me without scolding."

Five minutes later, Kondi knelt in the corner of their living room—not that a corner was a better place to pray than any other spot. However, she knew she was easily distracted so she chose the corner as her praying place where she couldn't see anything or even hear very much.

"Dear God," she whispered, "I know you love me. It's so easy to talk to you—at least when I know no one else can hear me and I haven't done anything wrong I need to confess. Please help Ulemu. I don't know what else to ask for her. She's unhappy and worried. Help her find her way out of her confusion. I ask this in Jesus' name." Kondi stayed kneeling for a bit with her hands folded and then rose to help her mother dish up the food for their evening meal.

"I need to talk with you." Bambo's expression seemed serious and he looked at Kondi beneath a cocked eyebrow. "However, we'll wait until after supper." He pulled out his chair and sat at the table.

Kondi looked at her mother with a what-did-I-do-now expression, but Mai gave her no clue to the difficulty. They both sat down too.

It was becoming a regular happening for their family to eat together, and Kezo joined them this evening. Ukhale lolled in the lamplight streaming through the door, but he didn't come into the house. He knew better.

"Kondi, will you pray for our supper?" Bambo still looked a bit stern.

She swallowed hard but folded her hands in her

lap and tried to pull her thoughts from her worry. "Dear God." She licked her lips nervously. "Thank you for our food and for Bambo and Mai's hard work to take care of Kezo and me. Please make our bodies strong and healthy. I don't know what I've done wrong, but help us to work it out so our family can be happy. Amen."

When she looked up, she noticed a little smile on Bambo's lips.

Mai turned her head, hid her smile with her hand, coughed and fussed with Kezo's clothes.

Kondi leaned forward and lifted the covers from the *nsima* and *ndiwo* serving bowls. Steam boiled up, spiraling toward the ceiling.

Bambo broke off a piece of the thick porridge in the central dish, molded it in his fingers and dipped it into the broth of the *ndiwo*. For this suppertime, the dish was mixed beans with a bit of onion, tomato and salt, and the flavor of smoke from the fire blended in.

Mai also dipped from the central bowl, then Kondi did too. Mai fixed a bit for Kezo, with a soft bean pressed into the porridge, but he fussed, wanting to feed himself.

"Don't touch your mouth with your fingers, Kezo," Mai admonished, handing him a small piece of cooled porridge. "Since we all eat out of the same bowls, this is important, and only polite." Kezo looked at his mother with his little mouth open, listening to her instructions.

When they first sat down to the table, Kondi had

felt hungry. However, now her appetite was gone. Could Bambo somehow have found out she was meeting Max at the crossroads? She was sure she had been quiet when she'd moved around in the house. Why couldn't they just tell her now and get it over with. Waiting with this hanging over her head—she couldn't eat. She pushed back from the table.

"What's wrong?" Kondi glanced from her mother to her father and back again. "Please tell me what you think I've done."

"We'll talk about this after we've finished eating," Bambo said sternly. "Now eat your supper."

Kondi broke off a piece of *nsima*, but she just folded it over and over again in her fingers without dipping it into the *ndiwo* dish or tasting it. The meal proceeded with Mai and Bambo making soft comments to one another. Kezo grew restless once he felt satisfied and wanted to get down.

When Bambo pushed his chair back from the table, Kondi hurried to bring the basin for him to wash his hands. She offered him the towel hanging over her arm. Next she went to Mai. When Mai washed her hands, she rose to go to the cookhouse to brew the tea.

Kondi replaced the covers over the two bowls of food, set them on a flat basket tray and carried the remains of their dinner to the cookhouse.

"Mai, please," she whispered as she bent to enter the low door of the cookhouse. "Why am I in trouble? I'm sure I can explain."

Her mother just looked at her soberly and shook

her head a bit. Kondi huffed out a sigh.

Mai opened the cupboard and brought out a small packet of biscuits—what their American friends called cookies. The soberness of her expression lightened as she placed them on the tray. She picked up the tray with the teakettle, cups and biscuits and the two of them walked back toward the main house together.

Kondi opened the door for her mother and sat at the table again. Mai poured the tea. It was milky and sweet, just as her family liked it.

Kezo squealed with delight when he saw the packet of biscuits. Each of them could have one.

She started to dip her biscuit in her teacup but stopped. *Mai doesn't like me dipping biscuits. I'm in trouble enough this evening.* She glanced away from her parents and out the doorway. The beggar boy huddled in his place under the tree.

Bambo cleared his throat.

Oh no! Here it came! She knew she was in trouble now!

"Kondi, didn't I ask you not to use grass from the cookhouse roof for starting fires?"

Uh oh! "Yes, Bambo."

"Why did you do it, then?"

"I only did it once or twice when it was raining too hard to find dry kindling."

"Once or twice does not make a hole in a roof." Bambo's voice took on an even more stern tone. "Rainwater floods into Mai's cookhouse now."

"I didn't mean to make a hole in the roof. And

besides I pulled grass from a different place each time so it wouldn't be noticed!"

"So it wouldn't be noticed? You were being deceitful, then?"

A flood of guilt and shame rushed heat up her neck and into her cheeks. "I guess so." She looked at the floor, not wanting to meet her father's piercing gaze. "But I can show you, Bambo."

"Yes." Bambo pushed his chair back. "I think that's a good idea." He pulled at her chair, too. "Let's go have a look."

Kondi hurried across the *bwalo* in the lemon light of evening toward the back of the cookhouse. "There . . ." Her look of triumph faded. *Maio! Did I do that?* A large hole in the dried elephant grass roof showed the top of the cookhouse wall. Only a few straggly grass blades dangled over the opening. "Bambo, I didn't know...."

"A hole is there!" he said, pointing his finger to the dark opening. "Holes don't just appear by themselves. Someone has to make them whether they intended to or not."

"Well, I didn't realize I was making a hole." She couldn't think of anything else to say.

Bambo cleared his throat, again. "One of my British customers has an appropriate saying: 'Little by little and the mouse ate the table.'"

"What does a mouse have to do with this?"

"A mouse doesn't. I was referring to the 'little by little' part."

"I only took some once or twice!" Kondi spoke

loudly—too loudly.

"Once or twice doesn't make a hole like that, Kondi." Bambo pointed to the corner of the roof. "In a storm, our pounding rains could ruin the mud wall without protection from a sturdy roof."

Kondi nervously plucked a leaf to give her hands something to do, and she stared at the ground. Shame flooded her heart. She tore bits off the leaf and dropped them at her feet. "I didn't notice I was making a hole in the roof. I must have used grass from the roof more times than I thought."

"Yes, I would think so. Little disobediences add up to a big problem." Bambo still looked stern in the gleam from the cook-fire coming through the hole. "Disobeying in little things is still disobedience, Kondi. It isn't important what size a person's disobedience is. Nor whether others notice one's wrongdoing. The important thing is to obey, even when you think it's silly to do so."

Kondi couldn't speak around the lump in her throat, so she just nodded her head.

"Tomorrow after school you will cut some grass and patch this hole. Do you understand?"

Kondi nodded.

"When you've finished, you need to call me to come and inspect your work." Bambo continued. "It will look silly, no doubt, to have fresh green grass on our roof when it's out of season for roofing a house. But, perhaps, since it's at the back of the cookhouse, no one will notice." A hint of sarcasm tinged his tone. "You know I like my property to look trim and tidy, so be sure to cut the new patch even with the edge of the rest of the roofline."

"Yes, Bambo, I will. I'm sorry I disobeyed."

Bambo's hand on her arm felt tight, but gentle, too. "Are you apologizing because you did something wrong, or because you got caught?" he asked.

Kondi rubbed at her tears, swallowed hard and looked at her feet. "Because I disobeyed," she said in a hushed voice.

"I scold you because I love you and I want you to do what's right, my daughter. Disobeying is never right."

"I know, father. I'll try to do better."

"Good girl." Bambo smiled and patted her shoulder. "And no more snatching grass from the roof for starting your fire."

Kondi nodded and ducked into the cookhouse to hide her embarrassment.

CHAPTER 7

When school let out for snack time, Kondi took her small meal outside and looked for Ulemu. She saw her talking with Max. Again? Kondi sauntered over.

"Hello," she said. "What are you two talking about so quietly over here in the corner of the schoolyard?"

Ulemu looked embarrassed and turned away.

"Don't go, Ulemu. I want to talk with you." Kondi reached out her hand.

Raising his voice a little, Max said, "You and Ulemu are close friends? I didn't know that."

Kondi faced him. "Yes, we've been close since we were small." She put a few steps of distance between herself and him. "Ulemu's not only my close friend—she's my very *best* friend. And I don't really want her talking with you on a regular basis. I think you're a bad boy, Max, and Ulemu's too fine a person to associate with someone like you."

Right away, Kondi felt ashamed of what she'd said. That was no way to tell someone they needed to do better. Her cheeks warmed with embarrassment, but Max just smiled and nodded as if she'd given him a compliment.

"You're a very handsome boy, but looks aren't everything. You need to change your ways and be kind to your friends, like the Bible says." Kondi suddenly realized this admonishment was only a little bit better than calling him a bad boy. Maybe Ulemu could help her. However, Ulemu was nowhere to be seen.

"Kondi," Max raised his voice to gain her attention, "I need you to do something for me."

"No!" Kondi said it with as much emphasis as she could muster. "Now you've made me miss being able to chat with Ulemu. And there's the school bell."

Max's forehead ridged up in a scowling frown. "You'll be sorry for this, Kondi. You'll be sorry you told me no." His hand went into his front pocket and he brought out his clasp knife. The blade flashed open. *Snick!*

Max was dangerous! Fear clutched Kondi's heart. She jerked around and walked toward the school building. She hoped Max hadn't seen she was afraid.

Later in the evening when she and her parents sat around the table drinking their tea, Kondi glanced out the open door. The beggar boy huddled under the tree beside the road again.

"Mai, the beggar boy keeps coming back to sit under our tree. Maybe it's the only home he has. He's been there off and on for several days." She pointed him out, silhouetted against the moonlit dry grass beyond him. "May I take him some food?"

"Of course. Better yet, have him come to the fire in the cookhouse. He can also have the last of the tea in the pot."

A minute later, Kondi squatted at the edge of the shrubs near the boy. "*Moni.* I'm Kondi. What's your name?"

The boy said nothing but with a stick he scratched J-O in the soil.

Kondi added an e.

The boy scratched it out and added an S-I.

"Your name is Josi?"

He nodded and motioned to his throat. A racking cough shook his whole body.

Kondi reached to feel his forehead for fever, but the boy pulled away from her. "Come, Josi," she said. "Mai has food for you. And there's hot tea. You can sit with us in the cookhouse and be warm while you eat."

The boy stood slowly. He swayed a bit and Kondi reached out a hand to steady him. His damp and dirty shirtsleeve clung to her fingers. As they walked toward the cookhouse, the light of the fire and the lamp inside quickly revealed his pitiful body. His arms and legs were gray with dirt and his torn shirt revealed ribs jutting out between sags of skin. His feet, caked with mud, showed a cracked and bleeding callus on one heel. Scabs made bare patches in his tangled hair.

Kondi's heart ached for him but she couldn't help staring. She'd never before seen anyone so dirty, so poor, or so hungry.

Mai smiled and briskly placed food, steaming from the pot, onto an enamel plate. "Welcome to our home," she said with a comforting look.

Josi just nodded and stared at the floor.

"His name's Josi, Mai." Kondi offered him the low stool she usually sat on, and she pulled a large stick of firewood from the pile outside the door and used it for her stool.

"Then, welcome Josi!" Mai handed him a plate of beans and *nsima*. Pouring the remaining tea into a tin mug, Mai added an extra spoonful of sugar.

Kondi glanced at her mother in surprise. To keep expenses down, Mai added milk and sugar to the tea when she brewed it in the cookhouse, so Kondi had learned to drink her tea the way Mai made it. However, since Bambo liked his tea very sweet, she brought sugar to the table so he could add another spoonful to each of his cups of tea. Now Mai was adding sugar for the beggar boy? Mai nodded meaningfully at Kondi and winked.

Josi ate hungrily, filling his mouth overfull in his haste. He glanced back and forth from the plate to Kondi and then to Mai.

Mai said, "Sit nearer the fire and get warm."

Turning to her daughter, she said, "Go heat a bucket of water. He can have a warm bath and wrap himself in this clean blanket until he's warm. We'll wash his clothes, too. They'll be dry by morning." She turned back to Josi. "I'm afraid you've been having a bad time."

Josi nodded and continued to eat, glancing from one of them to the other. When his plate was clean, Kondi noticed he'd saved a small piece of *nsima* and put it on the floor near his hand. He held the hot tin teacup between both hands, absorbing its warmth.

"He's soaking up warmth like he's been cold for a long time!" Kondi murmured.

She went outside and filled a bucket at the tap in the *bwalo* and set it on the fire, poking fresh sticks of firewood underneath. She took a half bucketful of cold water and set it inside the bathhouse. He could add hot water later to his liking.

When she went back to the cookhouse, Kondi noticed the small piece of *nsima* was gone from near Josi's hand. Ukhale sat by the door with a happy dog-smile, and his tongue lolling out.

Mai left Josi sipping tea in the cookhouse and walked toward the main house. She returned in a few minutes with some garments. "Josi, we—" she nodded in Kondi's direction to include her, "—Kondi and I sew clothes for people to buy. We'd like for you to have these." She held up a pair of navy shorts and a blue shirt just Josi's size.

Josi's expression brightened with delight, then dulled. He shook his head. "...no money," he said. His voice was so raspy he could only form the first part of the sentence with his lips.

"*Iai!* You don't have to pay. We're giving them to you."

Kondi smiled her approval. "Yes, we pool our money to buy the cloth. Mai cuts and sews the garments and I do embroidery on some of them, so they belong to both of us. I want you to have these, too."

Josi tried to say *zikomo*, but only a dry, pain-filled cough came out.

"I think he may have a fever, Mai."

"Perhaps. Let's let him bathe first, and then we'll see. Come," Mai said to Josi. She motioned to Kondi to bring the hot water.

Kondi picked up an empty bucket, filled it half full with steaming water, and taking the handle in her hand she snatched a towel from the clothesline.

"Our bathhouse isn't a house, really," Kondi chattered. "It's not fancy. It has no roof, but it's practical; it's just a wall of reeds surrounding a small space of ground with a large flat stone in the middle to stand on while bathing, so your feet won't get muddy."

"Here," Mai said. She slipped out of her rubber sandals. "Use my *pata-pata*. Then you can get back to the kitchen without getting your feet dirty again." She took the towel from Kondi and flung it and the clean clothes over the reed wall where Josi could reach them. Then she pulled a sliver of soap and a piece of sandstone from their places wedged in the reeds. "You can rub the calluses on your feet with this stone," Mai said. "Come to the cookhouse when you're done. I'll have more tea for you when you've finished."

Josi nodded, his mouth hanging open in awe as he looked from the soap to the steaming water.

When Josi finished bathing, he came into the cookhouse with the damp towel around uncontrollably shivering shoulders. Stopping in the doorway, he stared at the dirty clothes in his hand as if he didn't know what to do with them. A huge cough rattled in his chest and shook his thin body. He swayed with weakness and grabbed at the doorframe for support.

"Come here." Mai bustled up to take his clothes and help him to the stool. "Would you like another cup of tea?"

Josi shook his head. He stumbled getting to the stool.

Mai spread a *mkeka* by the fire. "Here," she said. "Come and lie down." She eased him down onto the mat, and tucked a blanket close to his neck for warmth. Mai felt of his forehead. Moving closer to Kondi, she whispered, "He's very hot. Go call your father."

Kondi stepped out into the dark night. Even though it was a moonless night, she could find her way by the star shine as she hurried across the *bwalo* to her father's workshop. As she stepped close to the door, she glanced through the window and stopped. The lidded box sat on the table in front of Bambo—

the same one she'd seen a few days before. It was open and he was putting papers into it.

She turned the door handle, but it was locked. "Bambo!" she called. "It's Kondi!"

"Just a minute!" The sound of Bambo's chair scraping the floor accompanied the thump of the box's lid and another clunk as if he'd quickly thrown it into a cupboard and closed the door.

Bambo flung the door open. "What are you doing here?"

"I'm sorry if I'm bothering you. I...I came to call you." Kondi's fingers found the knot of her *chirundu* and fiddled with it, adjusting it more tightly around her waist. "Mai wants you to come. The boy is sick."

"Kezo?" Bambo's voice rang loud with alarm.

"No, not Kezo. Josi!"

"Who's Josi?"

"The beggar boy who's been sitting under the tree for several days." Kondi pointed into the darkness.

"Oh." Bambo pushed his chair under the table. "Why does she want me?"

"I don't know. She just said to call you. I came as quickly as I could!" Kondi babbled. "He's very hot, she said."

Bambo locked his workshop door behind him, and then he and Kondi hurried to the cookhouse. But at the door, he hesitated at the opening. According to Malawian tradition, it was not a good thing for a man to enter the cookhouse. Even though Bambo loved the Lord and didn't believe in signs, luck and omens, tradition was hard to overcome.

Mai looked up from where she knelt beside Josi's mat. "He needs to go to the hospital," she said softly. "He's very hot and his breathing doesn't sound good at all." She adjusted a cool cloth on Josi's forehead. "I wonder if he has family nearby."

"I don't think so," Kondi said. "Until today, I didn't realize how often he's been hanging around our *bwalo*. He seems to be completely alone in the world."

"Josi," Mai said, gently shaking his shoulder. "Do you have family we should talk to about your medical care?"

Josi opened bleary eyes and shook his head.

"I'm not sure he understood what I said." Mai's features creased with distress.

Bambo still held onto the doorframe. He looked at Mai. "Who will pay for his medicines—and maybe his hospitalization?"

"Since he has no family, if the hospital doesn't have provision for people who can't pay, we will have to, I guess. He has no one else to help him."

For a full minute Bambo stood still, looking at Josi's shivering form. No one spoke. Finally, Bambo nodded his head. "I'll ask Chipazi if he will take us in his car. I can walk home if the doctor hospitalizes Josi." He turned and disappeared into the darkness to go and make arrangements with Bambo Chipazi for transportation.

Mai hurried after him. "You can't go alone, my husband. I will go with you. Kondi can stay with Kezo until we return."

Bambo must have agreed because there was a flurry of preparation to make the three-mile journey. Mai chattered instructions to Kondi while she was getting ready. "You need to be in bed by nine o'clock, Kondi." Mai shook an admonishing finger at her as Bambo Chipazi's car rumbled into their *bwalo* and up close to the door of the cookhouse.

Josi was so weak Bambo almost carried him to the car. Before Josi scooted to the middle of the back seat, he patted Ukhale's head. Then Bambo and Mai got in the car and sat on either side of Josi.

"Pay attention to the clock," Mai called back to Kondi as the car doors closed. "You have school tomorrow! And take care of Kezo." Even when the car began to move away, Mai continued to give instructions through the closed window glass, although Kondi couldn't hear a word.

When Kezo saw his mother disappear in the *galimoto*, he started to cry. Kondi tried to soothe him, but he sobbed and rubbed his knuckles in his eyes.

"You're just sleepy, my little brother," she said, rubbing his head affectionately and swinging him to her back where she tied him securely. "Go to sleep now. Mai will be here when you wake up in the morning."

CHAPTER 8

But she wasn't.

At almost midnight, Bambo's knock at the door had roused Kondi from a sound sleep. She glanced at the clock on the table where she'd placed it before going to bed. Easing away from Kezo, she sat up on her mat, peering through the glass at the top of the door. Bambo stood there alone in the moonlight. Kondi unlocked the door to let him in.

"Sorry to wake you. I forgot to take my key," Bambo whispered. "Mai stayed at the hospital to care for the boy. He has pneumonia and needs someone to care for him during the night."

Kondi nodded and sleepily went back to her mat in the living room. She wasn't surprised that Mai needed to stay with Josi. Many African hospitals had no feeding facilities and employed few nurses, so a family member or friend needed to stay at the hospital to help with the patient's care and prepare food.

Kezo stirred when she lay back down on the mat. She moved the blankets to cover them both, making sure his head was under the blanket before she covered her own. She heard Bambo preparing for bed in the next room and then the creak of the bedframe and his sigh as he lay down to rest.

Early the next morning, Bambo shook Kondi's shoulder. He whispered so as not to waken Kezo. "Get up now," he said. "You'll need to take food to Mai and the boy."

Kondi nodded and got up as soon as Bambo was outside. She dressed, eased through the squeaky door and headed to the kitchen house to make the tea. Half asleep, she filled the teakettle from the tap in the yard, set it on the floor and positioned the charred ends of the previous day's firewood between the three cooking stones of their stove. She walked outside for kindling and found only a few shavings, so she stepped to the back of the house and reached up to take grass from the roof's eaves. Suddenly, she stopped still and came fully awake. *I've done this so many times it's gotten to be a habit. It seemed like only once or twice.* She went back to the firewood stack, made a few more shavings with the axe, kindled the fire, and set the kettle over it, balanced on the stones.

Bambo came to the kitchen door but stopped outside of it. "You will need to take *nsima* and the rest of the *ndiwo* from our last night's supper to Mai at the hospital. Here's some money." He reached around the doorpost and handed her a five *Kwacha* note. "Take a couple of eggs with you and stop at the market on your way home to buy a chicken."

"Another chicken, Bambo?" Kondi asked, amazed. "We just ate chicken for supper a few days ago, you know."

"I know, but the boy will need meat to help him gain his strength, and chicken's easier to digest than beef."

Kondi took the bill and tied it into the corner of her *chirundu*. "I'll try to hurry, so you won't need to care for Kezo for very long."

"He'll be fine. I'll give him a half brick to push around like a toy car. If he tires of playing 'car', I can give him paper and colored pencils from my workshop."

Kondi's mouth fell open. Bambo was willing to let Kezo play in his workshop? She was hardly ever allowed to go in there.

She quickly gave Bambo tea and bread for breakfast, made the *nsima*, heated the left over *ndiwo*, and prepared to walk to the hospital. "Kezo's asleep on the mat," Kondi called to her father through his workshop door. "I'm going now. I'll come back as quickly as I can."

Kondi set out for the hospital on the other side of Dedza town. She stopped for only a minute at a vendor's stall to buy the eggs Bambo instructed her to buy. At the hospital, she served Mai and Josi the hot food she'd brought, but Josi was too ill to eat much. Kondi put the left-overs away in the cupboard by Josi's bed next to the eggs. Mai could easily cook those for Josi when he felt hungry. She washed the few dirty dishes at a tap outside in the sunshine. When she'd finished and stored the dishes in the cupboard, she said, "I'm ready to go home now, Mai."

"Please stay with Josi for a few minutes," Mai said, "while I go outside for some fresh air and a short walk about the hospital grounds."

As soon as Mai returned, Kondi headed for home. An uneasy feeling made her hurry. She stopped at the market to buy the chicken and almost ran the last part of the way. As she crossed M1, she glanced down the Ncheneka Road. The figure of a somehow-familiar man entered the elephant grass from the verge, and he clutched something in his arms.

Who could that be? It looked like he was sneaking something into the grass. Her unease grew into alarm, and she sped down the home path as fast as she could.

When Kondi came into their *bwalo*, Bambo rushed toward her, and he was scowling. "I thought you said Kezo was asleep on his mat when you left." He spoke crossly and loudly. "He *is* with you, isn't he?"

"No, he isn't, Bambo. I left him on the mat, just like I told you."

"Oh no!" Bambo gripped the hair near one of his ears in his distress. "He's not here! Not anywhere! I've been looking for him for the last ten minutes! I was painting and forgot to check on him before then."

"Maybe he's gone to the Chipazis' house." Kondi

started to go back to ask.

"He's not," Bambo nearly shouted. "I've already asked."

"Mai-o!" Kondi cried out. She snatched the *chirundu* from around her shoulders and, in despair, covered her head. "Mai-o!"

"Kezo was here just twenty minutes ago!" Tears splashed down Bambo's cheeks and he dashed them away with the back of his hand. "I hoped and prayed that when you came back I would hear that took him with you."

Suddenly, Kondi stopped still. She remembered Max saying, "You'll be sorry for this" and heard again the s-s-snick of the blade whipping out of his knife. The blood in her veins ran as cold as a chilly *chiperoni* rain. She remembered the figure of a man going into the elephant grass beside the Ncheneka Road. She remembered the shape of a man she knew—Max. And he carried something in his arms— something about the size of Kezo.

"*Bwerani*, Bambo! Come!" She whirled around and started to run back along the path from their home toward M1 and its junction with the Ncheneka Road. "I think I know where he is!" As she ran, Bambo thundered along behind her. They ran down the Ncheneka Road to the place where Kondi had seen Max go into the elephant grass.

"Kezo!" Kondi cried. "Kezo!"

Bambo pushed her aside and raced down a breakway in the eight-foot-tall grasses where the stalks bent back as if someone to gotten through there recently. "Kezo!" he yelled. "Kezo!" He plunged ahead through the grass that bent over his head. "Kezo!" Bambo bellowed in a terrified voice.

Kondi heard a cry, then a whimper ahead of them. Then a tiny voice called back, *"Abambo anga!"*—the polite reply Kezo was learning to say when his father called him.

Bambo and Kondi rushed toward the direction the little voice came from. The high grass stalks rustled—a rustle much louder than Kezo's little body could make. In a few more steps they found Kezo squatting on his heels, his little shoulders hunched. When he saw them, he began to cry.

Bambo snatched Kezo into his arms and held him close. *"Mwana'nga!"* He held his son close. *"Mwana'nga,* are you all right?" Bambo squatted right down and examined Kezo all over, asking him if he hurt anywhere. Kezo seemed fine, but he pointed his tiny finger to a scratch on his cheek, a long squiggly scratch that fingernails or a rough grass blade would not make. A trickle of blood welled onto his smooth brown skin and ran down to his chin.

Kondi plunged ahead following the trail of bent grasses that led her directly back to the roadside where she stepped out onto the beaten track. A group of people stood together wondering what happened. One of them was Max. He was just putting something into his pocket—something shiny, about the length of the knife Kondi saw in his hand at the school.

"Is something wrong?" Max asked.

Several of the pedestrians gathered around them.

"Yes." Kondi glared at him. "My brother was missing," she said loudly.

"I'll help you look for him," Max said, starting toward the grassy verge.

"There's no need." Her glare deepened. "We've found him now."

"Is he all right?" Max's voice sounded warm with concern.

"He's fine. He has a scratch on his cheek, that's all." Kondi turned to go back to her brother and father, but stopped at the edge of the elephant grass with her hands parting the blades. She glanced back toward Max.

The pedestrians told each other how dangerous it was to leave a small child by himself near tall grass. Max nodded, agreeing with them.

She stood still, her trembling hands parting the grasses. "He wasn't alone," she said loudly. "My father was with him, but he was sleeping in the house and Bambo was in his workshop. Kezo must have wakened and gone outside looking for someone to give him breakfast."

All the pedestrians nodded their heads in agreement. Children did such things. As soon as babies were old enough to walk, they could wander away.

"No." Kondi stared meaningfully toward Max. "He didn't wander away. Someone carried him."

One old village woman protested. "No! Who would carry away a child from the child's home *bwalo*? Every Malawian adult knows he or she is responsible for every child in the village. It takes a whole village to protect and raise a child. What you suggest is unthinkable!"

Max stood silent, rubbing his chin. He looked perfectly innocent. His hand slowly moved into his pocket and he showed Kondi just the tip of his knife. He winked and smiled.

"Yes," Kondi said. "It *is* unthinkable. But wicked people do wicked things. Kezo could not have walked this far in just a few minutes. He's a tiny boy."

Just then Bambo emerged from the curtain of elephant grass. Kezo, still crying softly, clutched his father's shoulder. A white trail of salt from his tears streaked Bambo's cheeks.

When the pedestrians saw how small Kezo was, they exclaimed that, of course, he couldn't possibly have walked so far in such a short time. But surely, no one would snatch a child from his own home *bwalo*. Such a thing had never been heard of before. All villagers protected everyone else's children as well as their own. How could such a thing be? Even people who did other wicked things protected the tiny children of every family in the village.

They may be surprised at this evil, but I'm not. I know Max!

Kondi took Kezo from her father's arms. She noticed a sticky drool ran down Kezo's chin. "What's in your mouth, Kezo? Show me," she said and held her hand beneath his chin. He spit out a well-sucked piece of candy into her hand.

"Where could he have found sweets?" Bambo asked. "We don't even keep candy around our house."

She threw the sweet into the tall grass at the roadside, and Kezo wailed. "Someone must have given it to him, Bambo, as bait to take him away."

Bambo shook his head in disbelief and one old lady clasped her head. "I can't believe such a thing would happen in Malawi," she said. "The old ways were good ways. Telephones and *galimotos* have been good for our country, but we should not have traded the old ways for new ones. Evil has come to our land."

Kondi didn't say anything more. Instead, she tied Kezo onto her back where he immediately quieted, burrowing into the folds of the *chirundu*-sling holding him there. She turned, glaring one final hate-filled look toward Max, and headed for home.

In the evening, Bambo and Kondi returned to the hospital, with Kezo tied securely to Kondi's back. She would take her turn, spending the night at the hospital with of Josi, so Mai could go home for a good sleep. They knew without asking that Mai was very tired.

"Josi is better," Mai told them when they walked into the ward. "The nurses have been giving him injections. His fever has gone down, but he's still very weak." Mai gave Kondi detailed instructions about how to take care of Josi and then she turned wearily to go home. "I'll be back tomorrow morning so you can come home for some rest, Kondi."

"*Inde mai*, but don't come early. Take your time to rest at home. I'll be fine here," Kondi assured her mother. They switched Kezo to Mai's back and Kondi watched them as they left the ward, heading for the warmth and comfort of home.

A bleak feeling filled her heart as she returned to Josi's bedside. Maybe Josi will be able to leave the hospital tomorrow. She and Mai would take care of him until he was completely well, but afterward, where would his home be? Sadness for Josi flooded her heart. He was so ill and would still be lonely, even when he was well again. Not even one family member to love him.

CHAPTER 9

Josi slept fitfully during the night so Kondi didn't sleep well either. She slept on a mat beside his bed on the ward's cement floor. When Josi needed a drink of water, Kondi brought it for him. If he felt uncomfortably hot with fever, she offered him a cool cloth. When Josi woke up and tossed restlessly, Kondi stayed awake with him, giving him bites of food if he felt hungry. Once during the night, Josi asked Kondi, "Is Ukhale getting food?" Kondi could tell his fever was making him say strange things he didn't understand or even mean.

As the sun came up, other patients' family members moved around, fixing food for their sick ones. The gentle clatter of utensils and chatter of conversation woke Kondi. She found sunshine streaming through the windows and Mai standing at the end of Josi's bed waiting for them to wake up.

"Good morning, Mai," Kondi said, her jaw popping in a huge yawn. She threw back her blanket and stood up. "Did you sleep well?"

"Yes, I did," Mai said with a smile. "Now it's time for you to go home so you can rest. Kezo is with Bambo, and they will be expecting you."

"Oh no!" Kondi hurriedly gathered her things together. "Kezo could get lost in the grass again, or someone could hurt him."

"Don't worry, Kondi. Bambo felt so frightened yesterday when Kezo went missing that he won't let his baby boy out of his sight today."

"I'm not afraid Bambo won't take care of Kezo, Mai."

"What are you afraid of, then?"

"I don't mean to distrust Bambo," Kondi said, clearing her throat with nervousness. "It's someone else I don't trust."

"Who do you not trust, Kondi? Is it me?"

"No, Mai, not you. I can't explain fully right now. It's just—I feel sure someone snatched Kezo from our *bwalo* yesterday."

"Pfff." Mai blew out a short breath. "I find that hard to believe. Malawians are peaceful, friendly people. We don't snatch other people's children from their own *bwalos*. Who would do such a thing?"

"I can't tell you, Mai, but I need to go."

"Well, don't try to go to school today. You're very tired with nursing Josi all night long. You must go straight home and sleep."

"I'll sleep when Kezo naps, I promise." Kondi bowed on one knee and took her mother's hand in farewell, as all Malawian children did to show respect for their parents or other elders. "Shall I come again tomorrow?"

"I'll send you word if you're needed. Perhaps Josi will be well enough to go home by then. Bambo will come to see us this evening, and he will tell you if you need to come tomorrow morning."

"I will take good care of Kezo, Mai. I won't let him get lost in the grass again."

"Of course, you won't. It wasn't your fault yesterday, Kondi. Accidents happen. Sometimes little boys just toddle off."

"I don't think he 'just toddled off', Mai. He couldn't have wandered so far in the short time he was missing. I'm fairly sure someone took him away." She left the hospital and ran for home.

When she neared the school grounds, her steps slowed, then faltered. Many of the schoolboys played soccer, rushing about the field and kicking the ball with powerful legs and sturdy feet. She'd never seen Max play with the others, though. Perhaps he didn't know the game. Her steps slowed almost to a stop as she gazed across the field.

"You're not looking for me, are you?" a deep voice asked from behind her.

Kondi gasped and twisted around. Max stood there grinning at the trick he'd played on her.

"You mean boy! Did you scratch my brother with your knife yesterday?" Kondi's face showed the fury in her heart.

"I could have," Max replied, "but would a nice person like me do a thing like that?" His voice sounded as slippery as the peanut oil Mai used for cooking. "Malawians protect everyone's children, don't they, until they're old enough to take care of themselves?" His tone sounded like he was repeating what he'd heard someone else say. He reached into his pocket and pulled out the knife—the one with the shining blade that flicked open at the touch of his thumb. "My blade will only do what I tell it to do—and only when I tell it."

"You're horrible!" Kondi's angry words seared the air between them.

"I'm not horrible when people do what I tell them to do." Max rubbed the knife on his shirtfront. "I'm very kind to people who obey me."

"I hate you!"

"I know you do. But even so, you will come on Friday night at midnight."

"No." Kondi's voice trembled with fear and rage. "Our family is caring for someone at the hospital. I'm needed there."

"But I need you more, Kondi." Max's voice was as light and smooth as oil floating on calm water. "I need you more than this sick person does."

"No."

"Yes, I do. You will give this paper to a man who comes to the crossroads at midnight. He will wear a red shirt."

"That's all?"

"Yes. You see it's very simple to obey me."

"I won't obey you. Get someone else to deliver your letter." She shoved his hand away and started to leave.

"No," Max said. "You live close by. You are the one to help me. I will be very kind to you and your brother if you do what I say. Otherwise..." He fondled the knife, its shiny metal glinting in the sun. With one touch of his thumb the blade flicked open. Chkkk! Max's smile only touched his mouth. His eyes gleamed cold as *matalala*—the pellets of hail that rattled on metal roofs and chilled the air. "Just so quickly your little brother can have another scratch on his smooth skin. Will the blade only scratch—or go much deeper?"

"You're hateful, Max." Kondi blazed at him. "And I hate you!" She snatched the letter from his fingers.

"Midnight," Max hissed. "Friday night. Don't fail." He spun on his heel and walked away toward the school buildings.

Kondi thrust the letter out of sight into the pocket of her half-slip and re-tied her *chirundu* more tightly around her waist. Her stomach felt sour and all twisted up.

"Hatred and fear are making me feel sick. Please, Lord, help me not to be fearful," she whispered. "Max is a very bad boy. Even so, I don't want to hate him." She sighed. "I know helping Max is wrong, but I have to protect Kezo."

She walked on past the school. In her mind, thoughts tumbled about. First, she excused herself for doing what Max wanted, and then scolded herself for her excuses. Her mind was such a jumble of thoughts she hardly knew where she was until she crossed to her own home grounds.

"There you are!" Bambo called from the porch of his workshop. "I've been looking for you. Please come and take Kezo so I can work on a painting. What's taken you so long?"

"I'm sorry, Bambo. I came as quickly as I could, but someone stopped me near the school." She picked Kezo up and carried him toward the cookhouse.

She spent the morning sweeping the yard, washing a few clothes while watching over her little brother as he pushed a brick around the *bwalo* making truck noises. At noon she carefully roasted two maize cobs and boiled some tea. She took them to her father in his workshop.

"I know you're working hard, Bambo, so I thought you would like to have your lunch here."

"Thank you, Kondi." Bambo seemed distracted and kept on painting without even looking at her. "Just put it there on the table. I'll stop to eat in a minute."

"Will you take food to the hospital this evening, Bambo?"

"Yes, yes. I'll go later. I'm busy now. Please, just put the tray on the table and let me keep working."

Kondi did as he asked and slipped quietly out the door.

Later in the afternoon she chopped a mixture of onions, cabbage, carrots and tomatoes to cook for supper. Bambo would take some with him to the hospital for Mai and Josi.

On Friday morning, the hospital released Josi to go home—but he *had* no home.

"You may stay with us for a few days," Mai assured him.

He dressed in his new clothes, but he was so weak from the fever by the time he finished he needed to rest.

Mai spread the *mkeka* she'd slept on in the shade of a tree in the hospital garden, and Josi lay down and fell into a sound sleep. Kondi and Bambo found them there when they came to visit.

"How will he find the strength to walk home?" Kondi asked her mother. "It's nearly three miles." She herded Kezo away from some boulders nearby. "Just dressing and walking out here has exhausted him."

"We'll have to walk slowly and stop anytime he needs a rest."

"He looks better, Mai, but he's still awfully thin."

"Yes, he'll need to stay with us for a few days until he's stronger." Mai glanced at her husband. "Your father and I have discussed this."

"What will happen to him afterwards, Mai?"

"I don't know. I'm sure the Lord will give us an answer to this question."

"I've been praying about his not having a family." Kondi looked at the ground and pushed a twig around with her toe. "Everybody needs a family."

Kondi felt uneasy when she mentioned praying.

She *had* been praying—but mostly about her own problems. What on earth was she going to do at midnight?

When they left the hospital, Bambo carried Kezo, and Mai and Kondi walked on either side of Josi to be sure he didn't fall. They walked home slowly as Mai had suggested, stopping often for him to rest. Once, they unrolled the *mkeka* in the shade of a tree and he lay down.

"I hope Ukhale's all right," Josi murmured as he started to fall asleep.

Kondi put Kezo to nap beside him, and Bambo wandered off to a kiosk nearby where roasted maize cobs scented the air. "Isn't it strange to hear Josi keep talking about Ukhale, Mai? He said some funny things about him when I was watching him in the hospital, too."

"He's been very ill. People do say strange things when they have a fever," Mai said.

Josi and Kezo slept for an hour. They both felt a lot more energetic when they woke up again.

They arrived home just before lunchtime and Mai unrolled the *mkeka* in the cookhouse so Josi could nap and keep warm near the fire.

Kondi closed the door to the chicken house long before supper was ready. Since all their work was running late, they sat down to supper well after dark.

Much of the daily work had been left undone while Mai watched over Josi at the hospital. "I helped with what I could do while I was at home. But it needs a mother's hand to keep things running smoothly," Kondi told her mother as she along helping Josi to walk across the *bwalo*. Mai carried the supper tray.

They all gathered around the table in the sitting room. Kezo, sitting on Mai's lap, was almost too sleepy to eat anything. After they'd prayed, Kondi pushed the *ndiwo* dish toward Josi, but he nudged it toward Bambo first. While they ate, Bambo said, "I have something I want to show Mai, and you, Kondi—something important. We will see it when we've finished eating."

"Can we see it tomorrow, Bambo?" Kondi asked. "I'm so tired and I need to go to sleep."

"Please forgive me, Lord, for this half-lie. I am tired, but really I'm just too nervous to sit around talking," she prayed in her heart. "I'd rather tell Mai and Bambo about Max forcing me to do things, but he's threatened to hurt Kezo if I tell. I have to protect Kezo. I want to get this midnight meeting over with."

"No," Bambo said, "I want to show it to you this evening." When they'd finished eating, he said, "Wait here."

"May I be excused to go lie down?" Even though Josi had napped several times, he looked exhausted.

"Of course," Bambo said.

Josi turned toward Mai. "I'll be glad to take the tray to the kitchen."

Mai and Kondi stacked the dirty dishes on the

tray and covered them with a cloth.

Bambo held the door back as he and Josi left the room together. Josi carried the tray of dirty dishes toward the cookhouse. Bambo went to his workshop.

"Since Josi is still coughing, I plan to check on him several times during the night," Mai told Kondi as they sat back down and waited for Bambo to return. They heard his workshop door squeak open and a bit later it squeaked closed again.

When Bambo came in the door, he held the lidded box in his hands. He set it on the table and cleared his throat. "I've been using this box for special papers. I keep my money in the bank in town, but in this box," he rapped on it with his knuckle, "are some important papers." He opened the box and took out a large sheet. It was folded over several times. He held it in his hand as he continued to talk. "My business has done well since we moved closer to town. I am very thankful to you, Mai, and to you Kondi," he nodded to each of them, "for helping me get my business started." He smiled at them both.

"Kondi, I'm sure you've been wondering what was in my box since you saw me once through the workshop window putting papers into it. Tonight, you will see one of these papers." He slowly unfolded the paper.

Why was he being so slow about it? Couldn't he just unfold it quickly?

When the paper lay opened on the table, Bambo rubbed his hands over it to smooth out the creases. "Here," Bambo tapped the paper with his forefinger, "is what was in the box."

Mai and Kondi leaned forward to peer at the paper. They saw straight pencil lines going this way and that. Some of the lines were broken with hash marks. Some lines came together at right angles and others seemed not to meet anywhere. Others had been erased and redrawn.

"What is it, Bambo?" Kondi asked.

"It's the plans for a new house—a brick one. I drew them myself. I have enough money in the bank to build a brick house."

Kondi and Mai stared at each other. Then they burst out with joyous, loud laughter.

"But," Bambo said, "I do not have enough to pay for the metal roofing. Look, here's the sitting room. These are the bedrooms, and this is the inside kitchen." Bambo pointed here and there, and the drawing began to make sense to Kondi and Mai. "Of course, we will need an outdoor kitchen, too, for the open-fire cooking," Bambo assured them, "which we can build out of bricks later."

"Would we have enough money to build a brick cookhouse for Mai and a workshop for you, Bambo, and put metal roofing on them, too?" Kondi asked. "They would be much smaller than the main house, so they would be cheaper to build. Then both you and Mai would have comfortable places to work."

Mai and Bambo shared a look of pride between them and smiled at Kondi.

"We have such a thoughtful daughter," Mai said.

Bambo nodded his head. "Perhaps. Yes, perhaps

we would have enough money to build the smaller buildings first."

"Wonderful!" Kondi exclaimed. "You and Mai deserve nice working places. Besides, our main house is still in good shape and the grass roof keeps the rain out."

"Perhaps that's because no one is pulling the grass out of the roof," Bambo murmured softly.

Kondi felt heat rush into her face, but she ignored him. "Then all three of us could save for the main house and build it later when we have enough money for both the house and a metal roof."

Bambo began to fold the paper into a smaller square again. "I will speak to the builder when I've drawn the plans for the two smaller buildings and see what he has to say. We will see." With a nod, he put the plans into the box and clunked the lid shut. "Yes, we will see."

Mai stood and reached to pick up the tray to carry it to the kitchen house. She stared at the empty spot on the corner of the table.

"No, Mai, Josi took it. Remember?" Kondi's smile held a teasing glint.

"Well, I guess I must be tired," Mai said. "Josi's a good boy to help with the dishes."

"You sit and talk with Bambo for a while. I know you're tired from caring of Josi." Kondi put pressure on her mother's shoulder, urging her to sit. "I'll wash the dishes and be sure Josi's in the cookhouse near the warm fire."

CHAPTER 10

Later, when the dishes were washed and everything was tidy, they all prepared for bed. Kondi unrolled her mat in the corner of the sitting room. Mai and Bambo whispered together in their bedroom where Kezo already slept.

It was amazing to think she might have her own bedroom some day. But tonight she had to protect Kezo. She had to do what Max wanted. So she couldn't go to sleep.

Her jaws popped with a huge yawn—as loud as a stick breaking for the cooking fire. Kondi sat up straight on her mat. Could Bambo have heard? She listened until she heard soft breathing from the bedroom.

Pushing the blanket back, she stood and walked to Mai and Bambo's open bedroom door. The luminous dial on the clock glowed in the pitch-dark night. Since the clock sat with the dial facing away from the door she quietly tiptoed into the room just far enough to read it. Ten twenty-seven. Kondi let out a breath, such a soft one it could hardly be called a sigh. She tiptoed back to her mat and again pulled the blanket around her.

Her eyes felt as grainy, as if sand irritated them. She blinked, trying to keep them open. In spite of her stress, her eyelids kept dropping closed. She flopped over on her mat hoping doing so would wake her up.

I must not fall asleep, she admonished herself. *I must not fall asleep.*

Kezo's whimpers made Kondi sit bolt upright on her mat. Oh no! What if she'd overslept midnight! She could hear Mai moving around in the bedroom, soothing Kezo back to sleep. Now how could she find out the time, with Mai awake?

Just then, Mai came through the bedroom door and crossed to the outside door.

"Is that you, Mai?" Kondi whispered.

"*Eya. Chete.* Be quiet."

"What's the time, Mai?"

"It's just eleven thirty. I'll be back in a minute." Mai carefully unlocked the door and slipped outside.

Now was her chance to get out of the house. Kondi slipped her blouse over her head, tied a clean *chirundu* around her waist over the half-slip she'd been sleeping in. She snatched a dark sweater from a hook by the door. Parting the folds of her *chirundu,* she felt in her half-slip pocket to be sure Max's letter was still there. It was. Pushing a rolled-up mat beneath the blanket on her mat on the floor, she stepped outside and hid behind a bush nearby.

Soon, Mai returned from the outhouse, entered the house and locked the door. Maio! Now, how could she get back inside once she'd finished Max's errand? An icy shiver ran down her back. *I'll just have to finish this job for Max and deal with being outside when Mai and Bambo wake up in the morning. I can sleep in the kitchen, anyway, even though Josi's sleeping there. I can't lock the door from the inside, but at least I'll be warm and out of the heavy dew.* She clutched her arms trembling with the chill—but mostly with fear.

She stepped around the shrub just in time to see an animal coming toward her across the *bwalo*. Her heart seemed to stop and a tingle of fear prickled over her tongue. Her hand clapped to her mouth and she darted back behind the bush. Parting the shrub's leaves, she could see the large animal still coming toward her. Bright moonlight gleamed on its teeth and its pink tongue hung out of its mouth. She was about to scream, when it wagged its tail, and she realized the animal was Ukhale, their own dog.

"Ukhale!" she whispered. "Come."

The big dog took a deep breath ready to bark.

"Ukhale! No!" Kondi hissed, stepping out from behind the bush where he could see her. "Come here!" She snapped her fingers to make him come. "Quiet!" She made Ukhale lay down in his place on the porch, and then she started down the path in the brilliant moonlight.

When she arrived, she stood in the deep shadow of a large bush and peered this way and that. No one was there. Was she a bit early? She hoped so. She couldn't be late! She waited a few minutes more. Then she saw the grasses stir on the opposite side of the Ncheneka Road. No wind blew, so it was probably someone moving there—or maybe an animal. She grasped the open edges of her sweater and snugged them more closely around her.

Suddenly, something growled behind her. She clapped her hand to her mouth to keep from screaming and jumped into the intersection. Ukhale followed her with his tongue flicking between his bared, gleaming teeth. Short bursts of menace worked around his fangs and escaped his mouth. Kondi blew out an exasperated breath. "Ukhale! No!" she hissed. The big dog growled again, glaring at the moving grasses beyond them. Kondi grabbed Ukhale's collar and dragged him back into deeper darkness.

A minute later, a man stepped out of the elephant grass on the Mozambique side of the track and stood in the ditch—a man wearing a red shirt.

Kondi's heart pounded as she and Ukhale stepped into the intersection too.

The man did not smile. His glance darted here and there toward every movement of grass in the wind. He looked behind him and then moved to one side to peer intently behind Kondi to where she had approached the road through the elephant grass. He took a step toward her.

Ukhale growled—loudly this time.

"Shhhh, Ukhale!" Kondi yanked on his collar and held on tightly.

"Who are you?" The man's angry words cut through the night with a hiss. He seemed uneasy and wary.

"My name is Kondi." She wished her voice didn't tremble, and she cleared her throat to sound more forceful. "I've been sent by Max with a message for a man in a red shirt. I suppose that's you." The sneer in her heart came through in her voice.

"Yes. Come closer." The bill of his baseball cap shaded his features in the moonlight, but Kondi could see the whites of his eyes glittering as he glanced right then left. "And leave the dog behind."

"Sit, Ukhale." Kondi released the dog's collar. Ukhale growled but didn't move until Kondi took the first step toward the man. Then the dog rushed forward, snarling, his hackles raised. "Ukhale! No! Go home!" Kondi shouted. The dog tucked his tail between his legs, and headed back toward home.

"Max sent me with this message." Kondi loosened the *chirundu* at her waist, plucked the note from the pocket and held it out.

The man looked left down the Ncheneka Road, then right where Mi made a black ribbon in the moonlight from north and south. He looked intently down the road to Dedza town on the other side. "Come closer," he said in a voice as rough as gravel.

Kondi took a couple of steps toward him.

He jumped toward her and grabbed her arm.

"Leave me alone!" Kondi jerked and tried to wrench it free. His grip hurt. "I'm just a messenger. I won't tell anyone who you are." She jerked again and again, but his grasp felt like an iron band.

Ukhale stopped at the entrance to their pathway. Kondi heard him snarl.

The man dragged her toward the elephant grass behind him. "Noooo!" she screamed as he pulled her into the swaying greenery covering their heads. The man grabbed the note from her hand, pushed her hard. She fell to the ground. The elephant grass thrashed behind her and Ukhale rushed past, snarling. The stranger vanished with Ukhale in hot pursuit. Kondi sobbed and fell forward amongst the elephant grass stalks. Silence fell over the dense African night.

The next thing she knew, several men appeared at the opening of the pathway to their home on the Ncheneka Road. She could see them through the stalks of grass.

"I heard a scream," one of them said.

Kondi clapped one hand over her mouth and the other to her chest to still the thunder of her heartbeat. She couldn't stay here! He might come back!

"Yes, I did too," another man said, "but I don't see anyone here."

But she couldn't go home either because she'd

have to pass these men. Kondi wiped her streaming tears, trying not to sob aloud. What should she do?

The third man made a derisive motion. "Have you been dreaming?" He moved to go.

Kondi peeked from her hiding place in the grasses.

The men walked around and talked for a bit. "Look! It's Chisale's dog, isn't it?" one of the men exclaimed, pointing further down the Ncheneka Road. He snapped his fingers for Ukhale to come. "It looks like he chased off a thief." Her neighbor pointed to a ragged piece of dark red cloth hanging from Ukhale's mouth.

Kondi recognized the rag. It was the same red as the shirt of the man she met. *Good dog, Ukhale!* Her hand trembled on the grass stalks she held back in order to view the scene.

"Good dog!" the men exclaimed. They knew better than to pat Ukhale or to try to touch him. Ukhale was a watchdog and trained to be friendly only to his owners. Ukhale shook his head, rattling his collar, and spat the rag onto the roadway. Then he wagged his tail and started toward Kondi's hiding place.

"No!" Kondi hissed. "Go home!"

Ukhale obediently disappeared down their home path.

Kondi's hand loosened on the grass stalks. Tears again sprang up and her breath caught in a silent sob.

It seemed like hours before Kondi felt she could step out of the grass and return home. She crept up the narrow path, holding to the shadowy side, and circled the edge of the *bwalo* to approach it from behind the cookhouse. Peering into the small cookhouse window as she passed it, she went on and tried the door. It opened with a squeak.

Josi sat up, rubbing his eyes. "What are you doing here in the middle of the night?"

"I got locked out of the house when I went outside, and I didn't want to waken my parents to get back in." *And that's honest. At least I'm being honest with Josi. Sort of.* "Go back to sleep. I'll just make up the fire, and sit here until morning."

"Just let me be sure Ukhale's all right," Josi said, starting to throw back his blanket.

"He's fine," Kondi replied. "Look, there he is by the door. He's guarding the *bwalo* like he should. You don't have to worry about him."

Josi lay down again and Kondi heaved a big sigh. It was going to be a long night.

Hours later, Kondi woke from a fitful sleep. Her hand went to her aching neck. She'd been dozing, sitting in the corner with her head propped against the wall. She rubbed her face.

Mai stood in the open doorway. Her eyes and mouth were round with amazement.

"Kondi! What are you doing out here?"

Oh no! I forgot about the mat rolled up in my bed. What am I going to tell Mai? Maybe—I hope—she didn't see it.

"I got locked outside when you went to the outhouse, Mai. I didn't want to waken you to get back in. You've been so tired lately." *That's true too. At least I'm being truthful—so far.*

"Kind of you, but completely unnecessary. Get up now and do your chores."

"Yes, I will." Kondi sighed with relief. Mai must not have seen her bedding.

Kondi hurried across the yard, shoved opened the door and nearly knocked Bambo down.

"What's the hurry, child? You could hurt someone." Bambo was often a bit grumpy when he first woke up. Getting whacked on the knee with a shoved-open door didn't help matters.

"I'm sorry, Bambo." Kondi's glance took in her bedding with the rolled-up mat still making a hump in the middle. "I'm in a hurry to get ready for school."

"Hmph! You're not usually in such a hurry for school. Besides, school isn't until afternoon, so what's the hurry?"

Kondi's heart clenched. Out of the corner of her eye she saw Bambo move on outside, still muttering to himself. Had he seen her bedding all humped up?

After Bambo shut the door, Kondi rushed to the corner where her bedding lay. She threw back the blanket, stacked the rolled-up mat in the corner, folded her blanket and placed it in the cupboard. Then she rolled up her own sleeping mat, stacking it beside the spare one. She let out a long breath of relief. *I think I've fixed things without getting caught.*

As Kondi washed her face and hands under the water tap in their *bwalo* and dressed for the day, she remembered an illustration Mai Mbewe had told them years ago when she taught their Sunday school class back in Ncheneka village. "When you tell one lie," she said, "you will need to tell another lie to cover up the first one, then another and another. Soon your lies will be strung together in a long line behind you, like a trail of pinching ants, one following the other. Don't tell the first lie," she admonished them. "Tell the truth."

As Kondi dressed, she glanced behind her to see if a trail of lies was following her. *Eee! I must be very tired after my scary night! How silly to look for pinching-ant lies!* Kondi headed back toward the kitchen.

"*Moni'tu,*" Mai said, looking up from setting the teakettle near the coals. "The tea's almost ready."

"*Moni, Amai.*" Kondi fussed with her *chirundu* as she settled on a low stool near the fire. She could feel Mai's gaze on her.

"What are you worried about, Kondi?"

"Worried? Why do you think I'm worried?" Kondi's pulse sped up. She knew she was not being totally honest.

"Your frown and fussing with your skirt tell me a lot."

"I'll be all right. I just didn't sleep well last night." *At least this is certainly true.*

"Yes, I thought I heard you stirring around on your mat. You aren't sick, are you?"

"No, Mai. I'll be fine once I have my tea and wake up. After breakfast I need to do some prep for one of my school classes."

"Since it's cloudy and cold, you can sit in here by the fire to keep warm and watch Kezo so he doesn't get into anything or burn himself. I need to wash clothes."

They ate breakfast in silence. Mai fed pieces of bread to Kezo and gave him sips of weak tea mixed with milk, but she kept glancing at Kondi with concern.

Kondi felt like "liar" was written in capital letters on her forehead.

In the afternoon, Max happened to meet Kondi where the school pathway joined the road to Dedza. "*Moni!*" He fell into step beside her on the wide pathway. "It's nice to see you. I thought you might not come to school today." He sounded like a concerned friend.

"Leave me alone." Kondi hissed the words at him.

She added "please" as though it was an afterthought.

"Now what have I done to deserve such a bitter greeting?" Max spread both hands palm up, speaking loudly enough for those around him to hear. Then he leaned toward her. "I saw you last night," he whispered.

Kondi flinched as though she'd been poked.

"You saw me?" she whispered back.

"Of course. I saw him take you into the elephant grass."

"And you did nothing to help me?" Tears of angry frustration sprang up, and she gulped to swallow them down. "I hate you, Max. You're the worst boy I've ever known!"

Max smiled and looked around as though she'd given him an extravagant compliment.

"I'm not a boy. I'm a man. And I was there." His knife flicked open and he slashed at a tall grass blade. It sank to the ground. "Don't forget." His whisper made her think of a snake's hiss. "Kezo is such a handsome little boy. You want him to stay that way, don't you?"

"Leave Kezo alone!" Kondi shouted. "And leave me alone, too!" She ran toward the school building, leaving him behind. At the doorway, she glanced back.

Smiling to himself, Max broke into a dance step, a waving grass head clutched between his teeth.

It was almost dark when school let out at 7:30 and Kondi headed across the playing field. "Maria!" Kondi called. "Let's walk home together." Apparently, Maria could not hear her with all the other children laughing and calling to each other. She continued down the school path. Kondi started to break into a trot to catch up with her, when a hand caught her arm, and a dark figure appeared at her side. She gasped and spun around. Max grinned at her.

"I told you to leave me alone!" Kondi's voice shook. She cleared her throat to control it and clasped her hands tightly together so Max couldn't see their trembling. "I hate you. I don't want to talk to you."

Max smiled. "But I want to talk to you. I *need* to talk with you."

"No! Go away!"

Max took her hand and continued walking with her like he was her close friend. "I need you to do one more thing for me. You will meet me on Friday night at the same place. I will take you to my camp at the base of Dedza Mountain. Then on Saturday night, you will meet the same man in the red shirt again and take him to my camp. After you've helped me, I'll leave you alone. You won't ever have to talk with me again."

Kondi made a bitter noise in her throat. "I know you. You're wicked. You'll just need me to do one more thing for you, again and again. You're a horrid

106

boy!"

As she struggled to pull her hand away from her, he gripped her hand painfully. "Don't pull away from me," he hissed. "You'll do this one more thing for me. Friday, you'll meet me at midnight. You will say the words, "*Ndine munthu'yo*" so I'll know it's you. Then on Saturday you'll meet the same man at the same place and lead him to my camp at the base of Dedza Mountain."

"No!" She pulled her hand back, but Max's grip was like a python's, growing tighter and tighter.

"Yes, you will. Remember, you have a handsome little brother." His free hand moved toward his pocket, where she knew the knife lay concealed—the knife that could not only scratch Kezo, but also cut him cruelly. "Like I said, I'll show you my camp." Max laughed loudly and flung her hand away from him, as though he'd been merely teasing her. "It's a great privilege to see my camp," he said in a voice as slick as warm honey.

Kondi started to run. She was going to have to tell Bambo about what Max was threatening. She couldn't stand this anymore. She sped home through the gathering darkness. *But I can't. If I do, Max will hurt Kezo!*

As if he'd heard her thoughts, Max's laughter rang out behind her.

CHAPTER 11

When Kondi dashed into their empty *bwalo*, she scuttled around behind the cookhouse and flung herself to the ground in the shadow of its wide eaves. Her hand clutched her chest, and her breath whooshed in and out. *I won't go! Max can't control me. I won't let him touch Kezo!* Then she bit her lip, realizing she couldn't guard Kezo every minute of the day.

A dark shadow appeared around the corner of the cookhouse. Kondi flinched.

"Are you all right, Kondi?"

The moon had risen, and Kondi could see the white ridges of moonlight reflected on Bambo's frown. "I saw you come running into the *bwalo* as if a *mfiti* was chasing you."

"Bambo!" Kondi exclaimed. She leaped to her feet. It was polite to stand when one's elders were present, but Max's implied threats still filled her heart with terror. She clasped her hands tightly to control their shaking.

"What are you doing back here?" he asked.

"I'm not taking grass from the roof for starting fires, Bambo." Her attempt at a diversion sounded weak even in her own ears. Had Bambo heard the tremor in her voice?

"No, I can see you've been sparing our roofline." Bambo looked up at the even edge of the roof. "You've fixed it well and have not pulled out any more." He looked at her intently. "I've been checking."

"*Zikomo*, Bambo." She started to relax since the conversation seemed more commonplace than she'd expected. She swiped at the perspiration on her forehead and chin.

"But you look frightened, and your hands are shaking."

Kondi jerked her hands behind her and clasped them so tightly her knuckles hurt. "A lorry hooted at me as I crossed the roadway, and I ran." Kondi's laugh sounded more like a crow's croak.

"Strange." Bambo rubbed at the stubble on his chin and glanced along the roadway. "I didn't hear a lorry hoot."

Oh, no! Kondi's mind scrambled for a way to cover her obvious lie. "It was a yesterday, Bambo. I just remembered it as I crossed today, and I ran."

"Hmph!" Bambo looked at her with a strange expression. "I wouldn't think a dash across the pavement could make you perspire." He rounded back toward his workshop, glancing back with a puzzled expression as he walked away.

Kondi stood stiffly until she heard the workshop door close. Her breath whooshed out, and she sat down with a thump. That was close! She sat in the moon-shadow of the porch for a long time until her heart settled, and her heavy breathing lessened.

"Kondi," Mai called from inside the cookhouse. "Come and help me with supper."

Kondi steadied the round platter while Mai dished up the *nsima*. But when she started to put a bowl over the tray to keep the *nsima* hot, she dropped the bowl on the patties and several broke in half. Mai frowned.

Then Kondi held another bowl for the *ndiwo* while Mai held the pot and pushed the beans into it. Kondi moved to put it on the tray. Just then she saw something move in the doorway. Something big. She dropped the bowl onto the tray with a clatter and rushed to the back of the cookhouse.

"Kondi! What's the matter with you? It's just Ukhale looking in the door."

Kondi felt her cheeks grow hot. "I'm sorry, *Mai*."

They wiped down the big tray where the bean liquid had spilled onto it. Fortunately, neither the beans spilled nor the dish broke. Mai covered the large tray with a cloth to protect the food from flies while they crossed the *bwalo* to the main house where they ate. Kondi reached to take up the tray.

"No, Kondi. I will carry it. You are having too many accidents today. What's wrong with you?"

"Nothing," Kondi replied, but she envisioned another lie added to the trail of them moving along behind her. She just couldn't tell Mai what's really wrong! She wished she could, but Max would hurt Kezo for sure if he found she'd told!

Kondi followed her mother across the *bwalo* and opened the door for Mai to carry in the tray. She brought soap and a basin of water to Bambo first so he could wash his hands, then to Mai, then Josi. When she put the basin in the corner she spilled water all over the floor. Kondi could feel her embarrassment rise as she went to get the mopping rag.

When she finally finished cleaning up the mess and washed her hands, she sat down to the table with the family. Bambo cleared his throat—he often did this when he had something important to say. "We will need to have a family discussion once the dishes have been washed after we eat. Now, let us pray."

The meal proceeded with Mai and Bambo talking together. Kondi couldn't say a word. In fact she could hardly eat. The few bites she tried to swallow would barely go down, so she finally gave up eating altogether. *Now I'm in big trouble*, she thought. *Which one of my recent mistakes will Bambo bring up to discuss?*

When the meal was finally finished, Kondi left Mai and Bambo talking at the table and she stumbled out with the tray.

Josi followed her to the cookhouse. "What's wrong with you, Kondi? You seem nervous or something."

Kondi just shook her head.

After putting the food away in the kitchen cupboard, she washed the dishes and put them to drain on the drying stand outside the cookhouse. Then, with a heavy heart she went back, sat at the table in the lantern's light and heaved a sigh. "I suppose I've done something wrong again," she said.

Bambo cleared his throat. "Mai and I have noticed you're not happy lately. You can't seem to concentrate on what you are doing. You drop things and have accidents because you aren't paying attention. Even though I find it hard to believe, Mai thinks you may have been going out at night for an hour or more at a time. We are both sure something disturbing is on your mind. What is it?"

Kondi's trembling hand flew to her mouth. She stared at the floor and nibbled the corner of a fingernail. She couldn't tell them. Max will hurt Kezo if she did. He had said he would. Kondi clasped her hands tightly together in her lap to control their shaking. "I'm sorry, Bambo, I can't tell you. Something awful will happen if I tell anyone."

Mai place a loving arm around Kondi's shoulders. "You can always tell your troubles to your parents, my child. We love you, and we will help you. Better yet, God will help all of us—together—to solve whatever the problem is."

They talked for a while, Bambo and Mai urging her to confide in them and Kondi refusing to explain her distress.

Finally, Bambo spoke sternly. "You *must* tell us

about this thing, Kondi. God tells children to obey their parents, so you must tell us. I will get police help if needed. We will help you and protect you."

"Oh!" Kondi moaned. "I'm not the one who needs protection. It's Kezo."

"Kezo!" Mai stiffened with shock.

Bambo grew ominously serious. "How can Kezo be in danger?"

Then the whole story rushed out. She explained Max was making her do things at night by threatening to hurt Kezo; how the man she'd met dragged her away and Ukhale saved her; how Max laughed at her the next day; how she felt sure, even though Max denied doing so, that he'd carried Kezo into the grass and scratched his cheek to frighten her into submission.

"He's insisting I meet him again on Friday for another assignment." She covered her face with her hands and sobbed. "Please, Bambo, help me! I don't want to do what he tells me to do again. Please, would you meet him instead?"

"No," her father replied, staring first at the floor and then out the small window.

"You won't help me?" Kondi's head buzzed, and the room tilted in the most astonishing way. "Please, Bambo!"

"Of course, I will help you, my child. And God will help us both so don't be distressed. However, you helped make this problem worse by not confiding in your mother and me, whom God assigned to protect you. Now you may have to take part in making things right."

The room continued to spin and tilt. Kondi dabbed at the sweat on her forehead, let out a long, slow breath, and lowered her head to her knees. Gradually, her thinking cleared.

Mai hurried to the cookhouse and came back with a damp cloth. She put her arm around Kondi's shoulders and offered the cool cloth to her distraught daughter. "Here, *mwana'nga*. Wipe your face with this and you'll feel better."

Bambo stood, strode to the window, and stared out into the dark *bwalo*. "I will see Maria's cousin, the policeman, tomorrow. The police will help us sort it out. I'm sure there's something more to this than Max simply frightening a schoolmate. Something sinister. Something evil."

"No!" Kondi wailed and began to sob loudly. "Please, please, don't go to the police. Max will torment me for the rest of my life. He promised he'd hurt Kezo if I told! Besides, I have to meet him again on Friday."

"Trust me. I've met with bad boys before—and straightened out one or two. Even so, this wickedness is worse than anything I've encountered before. However, I promise to protect you, even if I have to walk with you to school and meet you afterwards for a few days. Besides, I sense it's a police matter—something inside tells me so. We will trust God and take this threat to the police."

Mai nodded her agreement even though her eyes were large with alarm. "It's incredible to think any

Malawian would harm a baby! It's Malawian culture to protect children—everyone's children." Mai sat in stunned thought. After a few minutes, she shook her head and stroked Kondi's arm.

"But what about Friday, Bambo?"

"I'm thinking."

"Now," Mai said, "I'll fix us some hot tea. Bambo will find a solution and then we'll all go to bed. God will help us sort this out in the morning."

"But first, we will pray," Bambo said. He prayed for comfort and peace for Kondi, for wisdom for himself and the police when he took this problem to them in the morning, and for protection for Kondi and Kezo until the issue was cleared up.

Kondi felt relieved as she later rolled out her sleeping mat in the corner of the sitting room, brought her blanket from the cupboard, and got ready for bed. Before she lay down, Mai came in with a tray holding three cups and a teapot with steam spiraling from the spout. Kondi's eyes opened wide. It wasn't often her mother served her.

Sitting at the table, Bambo and Mai took their tea, and Kondi sipped hers while sitting on her sleeping mat. With her blanket wrapped around her shoulders she felt comforted and warm. She couldn't remember Mai ever before serving her like this except when she was very sick.

On Friday morning, Kondi woke early. The sun peeked yellow beams of light over the eastern horizon. Mist, like milk filling a saucer, lay in the bottomland, a tree or shrub poking up out of the white haze into the bright morning air. When Kondi let the chickens out, the hens clucked in glee, and the rooster announced freedom to the world. "*Kokoliko!*"

In the cookhouse, she started a fire between the three stones forming their stove, filled the teakettle from the tap in the *bwalo*, and set the teakettle over the open fire. She draped a *chirundu* over her head, wrapped the rest of it tightly around her shoulders and huddled close to the fire. She felt so relieved that she had told Mai and Bambo about Max last night. A sudden spurt of fear ran through her veins as she wondered what would happen that night and if Max would carry out his threat to get even with her. But then she remembered that they had prayed. The muscles in her shoulders loosened, and she swung her head left and right to ease the muscles in her neck.

After breakfast, Kondi saw Josi slip a bite of food to Ukhale. She smiled. Josi sure liked Ukhale, and that dog wasn't friendly with many people.

She helped her mother sweep the *bwalo*, put beans to cook over a low fire for their supper, and wash some clothes for Kezo. "I'll go to the market for you, Mai," she offered.

"I don't think we need anything today," Mai said, her face clouded with concern. "Until this problem's cleared up, I think it would be better if you didn't go anywhere by yourself."

"Well, I could fight back. Kezo couldn't. Something could happen to Kezo. That's my biggest fear."

Mai shook her head sadly and continued making *mandazi* dough. She would fry balls of the sweetened dough in hot oil and sell the doughnut-like treats to those who passed by.

At about three o'clock, it was time to go to school. Her assigned classes started at three thirty and continued until seven-thirty in the evening.

"I'll come with you," Bambo said. "I can walk with you as far as the school pathway and then go on to the police housing and talk with Maria's cousin. We need to resolve this problem as quickly as possible."

Kondi felt embarrassed. She was much too big a girl to have her father walking with her to school. However, Bambo seemed to understand and left a considerable gap between them as they walked along.

Max didn't try to chat with her during the day. He only winked at her at lunchtime. However, when classes dismissed at seven-thirty and she started for home, she found him lurking at the opening of the path from the playground. "I'll show you my camp tonight," he said. "Meet me at midnight at the crossroads. Stand in the shadows, and say, 'Ndine munthu'yo.' I will find you. Then you can take a man there on Saturday night." Then Max moved away to talk with someone else.

Kondi's heart stopped with fear until she saw Bambo waiting for her by the roadside. They walked home together, and when they arrived home, Bambo went right into the cookhouse with her. Kondi could never remember his doing such a thing before.

"Tell me," he said, in a worried tone. "What did this rascal say?"

"He told me to meet him again at midnight tonight. He's going to show me his camp at the base of Dedza Mountain. I'm to take someone there on Saturday night." Kondi began to shiver and rubbed at her arms.

Her father put his hand, warm and comforting, on her arm. "I will be nearby, Kondi. He will not hurt you." He stood and tightened his jacket around him. "I must return and make plans with Maria's cousin, Policeman Banda. He will know what to do."

"You must eat supper first," Mai said. "You may return very late."

He touched Mai's shoulder. "I will be fine for now. I can eat when I come home." And he slipped out the door into the darkness that filled their home's *bwalo*.

Kondi found it hard to eat, and she noticed both Mai and Josi ate very little. They put Kezo to sleep on a mat in the cookhouse where they could be near him.

After about two hours, Bambo appeared in the cookhouse doorway. "Our plans are made." He nodded his head. "We will catch this bad boy in his evil deeds." He laid a gentle hand on Kondi's head.

"You have nothing to fear, Kondi. I will be close by. I want you to meet Max at midnight as he told you to do."

"Bambo!" Kondi leaped to her feet. "You said you'd protect me!"

"I will, *mwana'nga*. I will be close to you when you meet him, and I will follow you to his camp. You will not be alone for even one minute. Policeman Banda will be with me. We must know the location of his camp in the forest so we can catch him on Saturday night doing whatever evil thing he's up to."

Kondi collapsed onto her low stool. Her hands shook so badly Mai rescued Kondi's sloshing teacup and set it on the floor near her feet.

"Wh-what will I do, Bambo?" Kondi could barely whisper the words.

Bambo squatted on his heels near her stool. "You'll do nothing any differently than you would do if you'd never told me about this. Just go with him wherever he takes you. Policeman Banda and I will be close by. Max will not be able to hurt you. We will follow you both to his camp.

"I don't know if I can do this. I'm so afraid."

"Then on Saturday night, when you lead someone there, we will be near, too."

"Saturday? Don't make me go to his camp again!"

Bambo laid a reassuring hand on Kondi's arm. "Once you arrive there with his friend, the police will close in and see what's happening."

"I can't do this. I'm terrified."

"Of course you are afraid. You'd be silly to not be

afraid. However, we'll need your help to arrest these men if they're doing something illegal. Remember, you've helped the police before so they could catch someone stealing a maize crop. You should be less afraid this time, since you know the police and I will be nearby to help."

"At least my ugly secret's out. It was such a relief to tell you and Mai what was happening."

"God will help you, Kondi. Remember the Bible verse, 'I can do all things through Christ, who strengthens me.'"

When Kondi finally fell asleep, dreams kept her tossing and turning on her hard bed.

CHAPTER 12

Kondi felt a hand shaking her and sat straight up on her mat. Her heart pounded like a drum.

"Get dressed, Kondi." It was Bambo. "It's almost time to meet Max."

Kondi's hands shook as she dressed. She glanced through the doorway of her parents' bedroom to the luminous dial of the clock on their chest of drawers. Eleven-thirty. She went outside to encounter whatever would happen.

When she walked into the darkened cookhouse, Josi's eyes were round like moons. Mai stood in a shaft of moonlight and her voice trembled when she said, "I will have tea for when you when you come home again, safe and sound." Mai meant to encourage Kondi with her smile and words. But Kondi could tell she was nervous by the way she kept biting her lower lip.

"Policeman Banda and his associates are already stationed near the intersection, so you'll be well protected. We will follow right behind you when you go to Max's camp, so don't worry" Bambo whispered. "Now let's pray."

Bambo took hold of Kondi's hand. He finished his prayer with, "Thank you, Father, for your help, and for your protection. We claim it in Jesus's name." Then he whispered, "I will go out ahead of you, so there will be only one sound of the door opening."

Kondi put on a dark sweater, then quietly opened the door.

Bambo slipped out first and stood in the dark shadow of the wide eaves of the cookhouse. Kondi went out after him and walked as steadily as she could across their *bwalo*, into the opening of the pathway leading past Maria's house, and on to the intersection. She glanced back once to see if Bambo followed her, but she couldn't see anything—not even a movement.

Just keep walking. Don't turn around again. Bambo said he'd be nearby and he always keeps his word. Besides, the police are not far away, and what's more important, God is watching over me.

When Kondi reached the crossroads, she stood in the moon-shadow under the mango tree where she'd stood before. From there she could observe the whole intersection. Her heart pounded so loudly she felt sure it would be heard. Her eyes moved back and forth, searching one place, then another. Nothing moved. She squatted at the base of the tree, pulled her sweater closer, and prayed, hoping she would stop shivering.

Suddenly, something moved down the Ncheneka

Road. Someone was coming—just walking right along—someone too small to be a man. When the figure came to the intersection, the person stopped and looked all around.

Kondi stood up. Her throat was so dry she needed to swallow twice before she could clear her throat as Max had instructed. But only a whisper of sound came from her mouth. She cleared her throat and said aloud, *"Ndine munthu'yo."* Kondi stepped out into the lighter darkness on the open track.

The small person coming toward her jerked and turned to run. "No, don't go!" Kondi said loudly. "It's me, Kondi."

The small person stopped. "Kondi? What are you doing here?" The person's voice sounded like Ulemu's.

"Mimi?"

"Yes."

The two girls hugged each other. Kondi could feel Ulemu trembling as much as she was.

"What are you doing here?" Ulemu asked.

"No, what are *you* doing here in the middle of the night?" Kondi pushed Ulemu back by her shoulders and then pulled her into another hug. "I've missed you so much! But why are you here? It's a long way from your home—and walking in the dark!"

"I was ashamed for you to know I was obeying Max's orders." Ulemu looked away in embarrassment. "That's why I avoided you. I was sure you could tell I was doing something bad."

Kondi hugged Ulemu again. "Max is a mean boy.

Has he been threatening you, too?"

"Yes."

"Me too." Kondi hugged Ulemu again. "Bambo will help us," Kondi whispered. "He has the p...."

However, before they could say anything more, another figure appeared as silently as a ghost out of the elephant grass. "Well," Max said softly, "what an affectionate meeting you are having! I knew you were friends, but I didn't know you liked each other so much." Max touched their arms with icy fingers.

A shiver crept up Kondi's spine, and she pulled Ulemu's arm into the crook of her own.

"Follow me now, and no talking." Max's whisper sounded bossy and cold. "I want to keep my camp a secret place." His voice sounded oily again. "Well, only my friends know about it, of course." In the thin moonlight, his teeth gleamed whitely through his parted lips.

Max set off at a brisk walk, and Kondi and Ulemu, arms linked, followed him. They crossed the M1 highway and, after a few steps, turned left, down a narrow, graveled track leading around the base of Dedza Mountain. The girls kept up with him at first, but presently Kondi slowed down a bit and pulled Ulemu back too.

"Don't be afraid," Kondi whispered to Ulemu. "My father's close by."

Max snarled at them with a menacing gesture. "No talking, I said." His voice hissed like a flicking whip. "Not even whispering." He walked on, now almost at a trot.

Kondi and Ulemu followed a bit further behind. Kondi squeezed Ulemu's arm, and Ulemu looked at her. Kondi mouthed, "Bambo" and pointed behind them. She hoped Ulemu was able to see her mouth in the pale moonlight and understood.

Before long, Max took a turn into the forest covering the base of the mountain. Here, under the fragrant evergreen trees, the moonlight was almost too dim for them to see where they were going.

Kondi was amazed at how silently Max could move through the dry grass, twigs, and small branches. They came to a footpath. Max turned onto it and followed it at a trot. Kondi looked back so she would recognize the spot on their return. Then the girls picked up their pace to keep Max in sight.

Kondi couldn't help glancing back every once in awhile hoping Bambo's sturdy figure could be seen following them, but she couldn't see anyone nor hear anything. *Maybe Bambo and the police aren't really there after all. Maybe we're going into the forest alone with this evil boy—no, this evil man!* Kondi felt her heart kick into a faster, more frightened beat.

Ulemu could hardly keep the pace, now, and Kondi helped her along.

Presently, Max motioned toward a huge tangle of blackberry briars and wild rose canes heaped up beneath the trees. He disappeared into a dark hole under the back of the tangle—the side toward the mountain and facing away from the path. Kondi pulled Ulemu to a stop, not wanting to enter the low doorway.

Max's head poked out. "Come into my camp," he said, not bothering to whisper now. He reached out and grabbed Kondi's arm. "Come in!" he ordered her. "Isn't this a great place? No one would suspect it's a room, would they? You both will bring the men here—the ones I tell you to meet. Don't be afraid. I won't hurt you now." He grinned at Kondi. "And I won't hurt Kezo—at least if you continue to do as I say." Max gave Kondi a sly look.

As the girls entered the camp, Max turned on a flashlight and shone it around so they could see inside. A room—not quite tall enough to stand in— had been hacked under the huge, piled web-work of briars. Poles braced up the roof along the edges of the room.

Max pointed for them to sit on the floor. "When you bring the men to this camp, you will not come in with them. You will only point it out to them and then go away again. Do you understand?"

The girls nodded in the gloom. Kondi whispered, "Yes," in case Max couldn't see well enough in this gloomy place.

The room smelled funny—a sharp odor. It made Kondi's nose itch. Her vision was adjusting to the darkness, so she could see bundles of leaves off to one side. A box and some packages of large, bulky envelopes lay next to one briar wall. Kondi only glanced at these and then checked to see if Max noticed her looking around.

"Now go!" Max ordered them. "And don't return here until you bring the man I send to you. This is not a safe place for you during the daytime. Come only at night, and only when I tell you to do so."

"Yes, we will do as you say," Kondi said. Bambo had insisted she say that or she'd give him an earful!

Ulemu merely nodded her head.

The two girls ducked under the low doorway, fled across the clearing, and rushed down the mountain path toward home.

As soon as the girls were out of sight from the camp, Bambo appeared behind them. He carried a brand-new, sharp machete in his hand. "Keep moving," he whispered. "I will see you safely to our house. The police will check out his camp once he leaves it to go home. Hurry!"

The girls began to run with Bambo right behind them.

As soon as they arrived at the Chisale's home, the two girls went straight into the cookhouse.

Mai had already started a fire, and a kettle of water ticked with heat, almost ready to boil. Mai made tea while Kondi talked excitedly of all they'd done.

Soon, Policeman Banda entered their *bwalo*. "I've left other policemen to keep watch at the mountain camp," he said. Even though he and Bambo knew men shouldn't be inside a cookhouse, both of them crowded in with Mai and the girls. Bambo pulled the door shut to keep out the night breeze, and the cookhouse soon warmed from the open fire.

"Now tell us," Bambo said. "What did Max say to you? And what did you see in his camp?"

Kondi explained to them about the room under the briars, the bundles of leaves, and the bulky envelopes near the wall. "I don't think he lives there, Bambo, because I didn't see any clothes or cooking utensils—not even a teakettle. I think it's a place he goes to for some special reason."

"Yes," Bambo said, "for a very special reason." He looked meaningfully toward Policeman Banda.

Ulemu said not a word. Her hands still trembled as she took the cup of tea Mai handed to her.

"Ulemu," Bambo said, "do your parents know where you are?"

Ulemu looked at the floor and tried to speak, but since her voice still didn't seem to work, she simply shook her head.

"I will go with you to your home as soon as it's light," Bambo said. "I'll explain to your parents what has been happening."

Ulemu simply nodded her head and gave him a grateful look.

Their tea finished, the two girls rolled out the *mkeka* on the floor of the cookhouse and covered themselves with one blanket to stay warm. Josi would also sleep on the other side of the room and Mai and Kezo would sleep there too.

The next morning, when Kondi woke well after the sun was well up, Ulemu and Bambo had already gone to Ncheneka village.

When Bambo returned close to noon, Ulemu was with him. They both looked rather tired, and Kondi felt a big yawn coming. Since they'd been up for a good portion of the night, none of them had slept enough.

Mai fixed them something to eat. Between bites of food, Bambo told Mai, Kondi and Josi about meeting with Ulemu's parents, and his explaining to them how Max pressured the girls into doing things for him.

"We will soon have this bad boy caught in his own trap, I think," Bambo said. "Meanwhile, Ulemu's parents have agreed that she should stay with us during the week. This way, she can have police protection and be close to school and whatever action will be taking place. She will return home on Monday, but this weekend she will stay here."

The two girls looked at each other with happy smiles.

CHAPTER 13

When the two girls awoke the next morning, the sun was high. Kondi sat up on her mat, rubbed her face and looked around the room. It seemed strange to waken with the midmorning sunlight streaming through the window, making a brilliant yellow square on the floor.

Ulemu sat up from the other end of the mat and asked, "Where am I?" She rubbed her face too and said, "Oh, Kondi, I couldn't think where I was for a minute. *Moni'tu.* I hope you slept well."

Each of them remembered their frightening trip with Max to his camp the night before. They threw back their blankets and rushed out into the hot sunshine to warm away their shivers.

"Did we really do that last night, or was it a nightmare?" Kondi asked Ulemu.

"We did it," Ulemu whispered. "Let's not talk about it out loud. The grass may have ears." She motioned with one hand toward the elephant grass growing at the edge of the *bwalo*.

Kondi nodded.

The two girls hurried to the cookhouse, knowing Mai would be keeping tea hot for them. They each ate one of Mai's delicious freshly fried *mandazi* breads with their tea for breakfast.

"Josi's feeling much stronger this morning," Mai told the girls. "Why don't you put a *mkeka* for him in the sun so he can warm himself?"

"What a good idea." Kondi reached into the corner for a mat and hauled it out the door.

Ulemu carried his blanket in case he felt sleepy. Kondi placed the mat in a sunny spot near the M1 highway and then they walked with Josi to the mat. Only the deep ditch separated them from the roadside.

"We'll sit with you for a while, Josi," Kondi said.

A group of rowdy boys approached along M1 highway.

Kondi and Ulemu recognized Max in the group and they knew some of the others from school.

The boys made loud noises and rude jokes as they pointed to the three friends on the mat.

"Who's that creature?" Hale shouted, pointing at Josi. He shoved one of his companions who pushed back. They laughed mockingly and pulled each other around, roughhousing.

Max shouted, "He's not a boy. He has rough gray skin like a lizard!" They all laughed and pretended to be frightened of this lizard-human.

Kondi leaped to her feet and bent forward, glaring at the rowdy group. "He is too a boy!" Her voice shook but rang out bravely. "He's my brother now."

"Hah!" Hale yelled back. "I've seen him sleeping in the grass and under trees like a dog. His hair was wild and long like an animal's."

Josi squirmed with embarrassment and looked at the ground.

"He's my brother—my foster brother. We didn't know he was our brother, but we've found him now." Kondi's voice shook with fury.

The young men laughed raucously, shoving each other and making ugly faces at Josi. Max yelled, "His legs and arms are skinny like ants' legs with knobby joints!"

"Yah!" Hale agreed. "Or maybe a chameleon!" They all hooted with laughter.

Kondi gripped her skirt—she was so angry, she needed something to hold onto. She shouted, "Do you even know what 'foster' means in your family? No. You are very poor if you have no foster brother. Your family's ordinary." She shook her finger at the crowd gathering. "Foster brothers are very special. You leave my brother, Josi, alone, or you'll have to answer to my father!"

"Kondi!" Mai called from the cookhouse. "Bring Josi and Ulemu. Come now, and bring the *mkeka*. I have some work for you to do."

Kondi started to roll the mat. She saw Josi stick out his pink tongue at the boys for their rudeness. She still wanted to smash one of them into the dust, but Mai needed her.

How unfair! With bathing, good food and the medicine from the hospital, Josi was gaining strength. Mai had given him a haircut and a jar of Vaseline to rub on his arms and legs. He was beginning to look like a different boy altogether. Now those nasty schoolboys didn't have a reason to tease her new foster brother.

"I wish we didn't have to go to school today," Kondi said to Ulemu that afternoon, as they ate a snack together in the shade. Since Josi sat nearby, Kondi couldn't say anything further, but she looked meaningfully at Ulemu.

Ulemu nodded. She understood. "Me too." She shifted on the tree root where they sat. "I'll be very glad when tomorrow's over."

"Yes, the day after tomorrow will be a very good day." Kondi nodded solemnly.

Josi's cough was almost gone and his skin, hair and the whites of his eyes looked clear and healthy. He still hadn't regained all the strength he needed, but he smiled more often and moved with greater ease and energy. Good food, cleanliness, and plenty of sleep were giving his body a chance to heal. Now, he cocked an eyebrow at the girls as if they were acting strangely.

"Come, girls," Mai called. "I need you to go to the market to buy some dried fish for supper. "Hurry now, so you won't be late for school this afternoon," Mai said.

Josi watched the girls closely, as they headed down the path toward town, whispering together and hurrying along. When they were out of sight, he patted Ukhale's head and gave him a bite of bread. Then he headed for the cookhouse with Ukhale at his heels. "What's wrong with Kondi and Ulemu?" he asked Mai.

Mai darted a glance at him but continued chopping tomatoes and onions to go with the fish she would cook for their supper. "I think they are all right," she said. "Why do you ask?"

"They talked funny at breakfast." Josi squatted near the cooking fire and leaned over to add another stick of firewood. "Like they didn't want me know what they meant."

"They'll be fine, Josi. We pray for them every day, don't we? God will watch over them and protect them."

Josi's head came up. "Protect them?" He stood and leaned against the edge of the doorframe. "Do they need protection?"

Mai swallowed hard at her mistake. "They will be all right, Josi. Don't worry about them."

Josi picked up the broom. It was just rough brush tied together with string. "I'll sweep the *bwalo* for you, Mai. It's time I began to help around here." But as he started sweeping near Bambo's workshop, he felt troubled.

People walking past Bambo's workshop liked to stop in the shade of the porch and finish chewing their sugar cane or eating the roasted corn they knuckled off the cob. Unfortunately, before they continued their journey, they spat out the sugar cane pith in the rain gutter and dropped the empty corncobs in the yard.

When Josi neared the window, he glanced up. The window was open just a crack. He could hear Bambo talking with someone in low tones.

Knowing he shouldn't listen, he was just about to turn away when he heard the words *tonight* and *midnight* and Kondi and Ulemu's names. He knew something was wrong. Kondi and Ulemu hadn't seemed happy when they left for town. He wondered what was going on.

He continued to sweep away from the workshop with even more energy. The brush broom rattled loudly, but the noise wasn't able to override the voice of Bambo's guest, Policeman Banda. Josi stopped sweeping for a minute and then began to sweep back toward the workshop. What he heard made his skin prickle and the hair at the back of his neck stand up. He determined to stay awake tonight. He'd help Bambo, Kondi, and Ulemu when they went out around midnight.

Later in the afternoon, the aroma of dried fish stewing wafted across the *bwalo* on every drift of breeze. Josi felt pleased with the job he'd finished. He had been able to sweep the entire yard, even though he needed to rest a couple of times.

When the girls came from school and Bambo came from his workshop to eat supper, he stopped in the doorway. His index finger circled, pointing to the whole *bwalo*. "Josi," he said, "you've done a very good job. Thank you. I hope you haven't tired yourself too much."

Josi felt his heart swell with pride. He hadn't received many compliments in his life. It felt good to be praised. Even though he liked Bambo's thanks for his help, he felt warmth creep up his neck.

"*Zikomo*," he said. "Even though I'm still tired, I need to start helping with the work since I'm feeling better."

Bambo smiled and patted his shoulder. "I'm glad you want to help," he said. "But start by doing a little bit at a time. We don't want you to take a turn for the worse."

Bambo entered the main house and Josi followed him inside. After Bambo was seated, Josi sat down. It was only respectful to let adults sit down first.

When the rest of the family came in and sat down, Bambo cleared his throat like he always did before he started to say the blessing over their food. Instead, he said, "We like having you around here, Josi, not because of the work you would do but just because we like you. You are wanted for yourself. We want you to stay here and be like our son. Would you like that?"

Josi could feel the sting of tears forming in his eyes. He blinked hard against it. *Don't cry. Don't cry!* Men didn't cry, did they? He gulped at the big lump in his throat.

"Yes," he said. "Yes, I'd like very much to be your son. I'll try to be as good to you as you've been to me."

"That's wonderful!" Bambo said, smiling broadly. "Now shall we pray?"

After supper, the Chisales sat around a fire in their *bwalo*. Mai roasted cobs of corn in the coals, carefully turning each one. Then she handed a cob to each of the family, including Ulemu.

Kondi accepted hers but she just rotated it in her hand. Out of the corner of her eye, she saw Josi silently slip from the cookhouse and squat behind her mother.

"Josi!" Mai called. "The roasted maize is ready!"

"I'm here, Amai," Josi said.

Mai jumped with a start. "I didn't see you come. I didn't even hear you. You move so quietly." She turned to the girls. "Eat your maize, girls. Then you must go to bed early." She glanced around the *bwalo*, as if searching every corner and taking note of every moving blade of elephant grass. Ulemu plucked at the edges of her *chirundu* and examined the *bwalo* too.

Mai whispered, "You need to be rested for your adventure tonight."

Kondi shifted on her stool. "I don't really want to do this, Mai."

Josi's attention moved from one to another as they spoke. He was so quiet no one even realized he listened.

Mai nodded. "I understand. But you do want to bring this boy to justice, don't you?"

"Yes." Kondi looked into the coals and pushed a stick of firewood further between the stones. A tongue of flame burst up. "Of course I do. But I'm afraid."

"I am too," Ulemu said. "Can't we just let the police handle it?" She nervously plucked a few grains of corn from her cob and popped them into her mouth.

"They could do it alone, but they need your help to be sure they catch this boy in whatever he's doing wrong."

"Don't worry, girls," Bambo said. "The police will be already in place at his camp by sundown. And I will be with you. I promise not to leave you for one minute. You will go ahead with Max's 'guests', and I will be directly behind all of you."

"But sometimes things don't go the way you think they will, even when you plan well."

"That's true, Kondi. But you will have the courage to do your part to help—I know you will."

"Courage?" Kondi laughed at herself. "I don't feel courageous at all."

"I don't either," Ulemu said. Her voice sounded tearful. "How do we find courage?"

"To have courage doesn't mean that you have no fear. Being courageous means that you do what's right in spite of your fears."

Kondi nodded and Ulemu looked thoughtful. The two girls set what was left of their roasted corn cobs back on the plate.

"I will waken you at eleven-thirty, so go right to sleep," Bambo said.

The girls nodded, agreeing with what he said, and went off to the main house to prepare for bed. But how could a person sleep when they each knew frightening events were about to happen?

"I know your mother and father mean to comfort us, Kondi," Ulemu said as she helped Kondi roll out their mat. "But I don't think I'll be able to sleep at all, do you?"

"I doubt that I will, either," Kondi replied.

The girls didn't undress before lying on the mat since they felt sure they would be flustered when they got up again in the middle of the night.

Kondi settled her blanket around her, assuming she'd just lie there and stare into the darkness. Ulemu lay down, too, and pulled her blanket over her head. Kondi could hear Ulemu whispering prayers in the darkness for a long time. Kondi echoed those prayers in her own heart.

"Kondi!" Bambo's whisper brought his daughter from a sound sleep. "It's eleven-thirty. Time to get up."

"Hmmm?" Kondi threw the blanket off and rubbed her nose. "Oh!" She pushed the blanket away and jumped up. "Is it time to go already?"

"Shhh!" Bambo admonished. "Whisper. We don't want anyone to hear us talking together."

Kondi shook Ulemu's shoulder. "Mimi, wake up!"

Ulemu leaped to her feet.

Josi opened the door, and Mai came through with cups and the teakettle on a tray. "A good cup of hot tea will help you get a good start." The five of them stood in the pitch darkness near the table sipping tea. They didn't want to light a candle or sit down because a light and the noise of chairs scraping on the floor might alert Max's "guests" that others, besides the girls, were awake.

Before they'd emptied their cups, Kondi's and Ulemu's hands shook so badly they needed to set their teacups on the table. Each girl put on a warm, dark sweater and buttoned it up to her neck.

"Now," Bambo whispered, "let's pray before we start out."

They all bowed their heads and Bambo's whispered prayer carried through the room. "Our Father, we ask for protection for everyone involved in tonight's venture. Help us, Father, to bring justice to those who don't obey the Malawi's laws. Give each of us your courage and strength of character, and please keep each of us safe. We pray these things in Jesus's name."

"Thank you, Bambo. I feel better now," Kondi whispered in the darkness.

Bambo opened the door for the girls. "I'll be right behind you all the way," he said in a low tone. Then he laid his hand on Kondi's arm. "If the men should try to take you away, fall to the ground. You'll be harder to kidnap if you fall limp. We'll come to help as soon as we can."

"Bambo!" Kondi's alarm at this thought made her speak aloud.

"Shhh!" Bambo laid a sturdy finger over Kondi's lips. "Remember. Fall to the ground." His whisper was only a warm breath by her ear. Bambo pushed the two girls gently toward the door.

The girls stepped out and started across the bwalo. They heard the door shut silently behind them. Kondi glanced back to see if Bambo followed them, but she couldn't see him anywhere. Bambo had said he'd be right behind them. She took Ulemu's hand and they walked together down the path toward Ncheneka Road and the intersection with M1.

By the time the girls reached the moon-shadow of the huge mango tree, their feet and the hems of their wrap skirts were drenched from the grass bent heavy with dew along their path. Kondi could feel the shiver in Ulemu's hand, trembling with the night's chill and with fear rushing along in her blood. Kondi shivered too.

They stopped beneath the mango and peered through the elephant grass lining both the tarred roadway and the dirt road crossing it. Nothing moved. Only the elephant grass swayed in the night's breeze.

Kondi put her cheek close to Ulemu's. "I don't see anyone, do you?"

"No, I don't." Ulemu's whisper sounded dry and thready. "Let's just go back home." She turned to go. "Nobody's coming."

At one spot Kondi noticed the elephant grass moving like someone was trying to walk through it. She clutched Ulemu's arm.

"What?" Ulemu's whisper seemed loud in the quiet of the night. "Let's g—" She looked back, her eye following to where Kondi pointed, and gasped for air. A man wearing a red shirt stepped onto the dirt surface of Ncheneka Road, peering left and right. Ulemu crouched to the ground, attempting to hide even though the black shadow of the mango tree hid them well.

"It's time now, Mimi." Kondi took Ulemu's hand and steadied her as she got to her feet. Together they stepped out from the dark shadow into the white moonlight. "We're here," she said aloud.

The man whipped around and stared at them for a minute. Kondi noticed there was a big hole in his red shirtsleeve. Good for Ukhale!

"Why two? I was told to meet only one girl."

"I think Max may have another 'guest' coming," Kondi said. "Look!" She pointed further along where another man was making his way toward them. In the moonlight, she could barely make out his dark shirt striped with narrow bars of white.

"No," said the first man. "I wasn't told there would be several of us."

"I don't think Max meant for you to arrive together," Kondi said. She pointed to her friend. "Ulemu was supposed to meet one of you and I would meet the other. However, together we can take you to Max's camp."

She glanced back toward where their home path intersected with Ncheneka Road to try to see Bambo behind them. No one was there. There wasn't even any movement in the dark opening of the pathway.

Bambo's got to be nearby! Kondi took Ulemu's hand, and they started off. Trusting wasn't easy. She needed to just trust God and Bambo, too.

In less than a minute, the four of them crossed M1, the girls leading and the men coming along behind. They walked about twenty yards towards Dedza town, and made a left turn onto the graveled track winding around the base of the mountain.

Ulemu made no sound and hung back against Kondi's grasp. "Come on, Mimi!" Kondi whispered in her ear. "We need to do this together. Remember, we're protected." She pointed a thumb over her shoulder and a finger toward the sky.

Ulemu quickened her pace, and Kondi could see the quick gleam of her teeth as she gave a shaky smile.

They soon came to the unmarked path leading

away from the graveled track, really only a spot of trampled grass, not a proper path at all. "We go through here," Kondi whispered to the two men. The men stopped for a minute, whispered together, and then followed behind the two girls.

Before leaving the grasslands behind as they climbed the first gentle slopes at the foot of Dedza Mountain, Kondi glanced behind several times to try to see Bambo. She saw nothing. When they entered the pine forest, walking was more dangerous because of fallen branches and piles of evergreen boughs. They began to be a bit breathless from climbing the slope and stepping high over debris. Kondi stumbled to a halt to catch her breath.

The two men whispered together, pointing up the pathway, and shoved the girls ahead of them.

Again, Kondi glanced behind for Bambo. However, here under the dense canopy of the pine forest, darkness made it nearly impossible to see more than a few feet in any direction. Even the two men walking behind them seemed to be only moving shapes as dark as the tree trunks around them.

One of the men pushed hard on Kondi's shoulder. "Go!" He whispered near her ear.

Kondi stumbled, but Ulemu's grip saved her from falling.

The two girls led on until they came to a corner where the path twisted toward the heaped pile of briars under which Max made his camp.

"It's there," Kondi said, pointing. "His camp's under those briars. The door's at the back where it can't be seen from here. You can find it easily." She and Ulemu started to retreat.

"No!" one of the men said aloud. "You're not leaving." He grabbed Kondi's arm, and the other man caught Ulemu's so they couldn't run. "You will stay with us and take us back."

"*Iai!*" Kondi said loudly, jerking against his grip. "No! Max told us just to show you the place. He didn't say we should stay with you and show you the way back. We're going now!" She twisted hard against the man's grasp on her arm.

His hand clamped even more tightly. "Stop! You must come with us," he hissed.

Something moved near the heap of briars. Kondi's heart raced with fear.

"Quiet!" a voice said softly. "I'm Max. Welcome to my camp."

CHAPTER 14

As Max moved a hanging blanket aside from the doorway for them to enter his briar hut,

the dim light of a candle gleamed through the opening.

The man holding her arm pushed Kondi forward. *Yesu!* she cried in her heart. Ulemu and her captor followed. *Yesu!* Her heartbeat hammered loudly in her own ears.

"Hello, Kondi." Max's voice was soft but menacing. "Hello, Ulemu. You girls have done me a great favor. Thank you." He mockingly bowed low and every word held sarcasm.

Neither of the girls said a word. The men thrust them forward so hard they stumbled into the makeshift room and fell to the ground in the furthest spot from the door. As they fell, a strange and acrid odor wafted up from a pile of leaves onto which the girls fallen.

The three men squatted together, blocking the doorway, and began to converse in a dialect the girls didn't understand. The single candle's light wavered in the gust of air blowing through the door.

Dear God, how can Bambo help us now? He expected the men to let us go so we could return home. Jesus, help us!

Kondi's heart thundered loudly in her chest. Surely the men could hear it! She glanced over her shoulder at Ulemu, crouched behind her. In the dim light, Kondi could see her lips moving but no words could be heard.

Suddenly, the men finished talking. All three stood together. Money changed hands. Max gave them some of the packages from behind the pile of leaves and opened the box to hand them other bundles. The men nodded to one another and the strangers started toward the door.

Kondi and Ulemu stood up, preparing to leave behind them. "No," Max hissed. "You stay here!" Behind the men, he leaped across the doorway with his arms spread wide to prevent their exit.

"We've done what you said," Kondi said loudly. "Now let us go!"

"No!" Dim reflections of light rippled on the ridges of Max's menacing scowl. The girls could see little else in the dim room.

"No!" Max repeated. "You will both come with me further up the mountain. I have something to show you up there."

A chill of fear ran up Kondi's spine. There was nothing up the mountain but more trees and briars. She tried to shout that they wouldn't go but her dry throat made no sound. She shook her head, forgetting Max could barely see her. She swallowed to moisten her mouth. Her gulp sounded loudly in the darkness. "No," she whispered. "No, we won't go."

Max grabbed Kondi's arm. He reached behind her for Ulemu's, but she scooted behind Kondi's back.

"Come here!" Max demanded.

"No!" Ulemu shouted. "I won't!"

Kondi remembered her father's last admonition.

"Mimi, fall down!" Kondi yelled. "Fall down!"

Both girls fell to the floor of the camp. Max got hold of Ulemu's arm, but he couldn't drag both girls through the doorway at the same time.

"Get up!" Max shouted.

Suddenly, something crashed in the underbrush outside. An authoritative voice shouted, "Come out!"

Max dropped both girls' arms. Leaping across the room, he grabbed his machete. In the candlelight, his huge knife flashed a wicked-looking, razor-sharp blade.

Suddenly, a huge dark figure leaped through the doorway toward Max. Both men gripped the machete's handle. Grunts of struggle filled the air as they thrashed about.

Ulemu ran out the door into the arms of a policeman. Kondi started to follow but she stopped short when she heard her father's voice order, "Drop the machete, Max."

"Leave my father alone!" Kondi shouted, turning back. She pounded on the back of the struggling figure in front of her.

"Kondi, leave!" Bambo's voice sounded from right under her hand.

A sweeping hand shoved Kondi aside and she crashed against the rough thorny wall of the camp, cutting her arm on the briars. She felt a spare axe handle leaning against the wall. Snatching it, she leaped toward the struggling figures in the darkness.

"Leave my father alone, Max!" she shouted. She whacked with her weapon. Hard!

"Kondi, no!" Bambo yelped. "You hit *me!*"

"Oh no!" Kondi stopped dead still.

As Max tried to get away from Bambo's grip, the two men moved closer toward the door. In the thin moonlight filtering through the trees, Kondi could now tell which man which. She raised her stick and bought it down hard on Max's head.

Max sank to the floor with a moan.

Bambo stood, panting and rubbing his shoulder as Max writhed in pain on the floor. Two policemen leaped through the doorway and pinned Max's arms behind him. She could hear the rattle and snap of handcuffs.

"Now, let's see what you have in your camp, Max." One of the policemen lit his brilliant flashlight and began searching among the dried leaves near the wall.

"Good job, Kondi!" her father said with a smile. "Even though you almost knocked out your own father!" He rubbed his shoulder. In the leaping light from the policeman's bright flashlight she could see the white gleam of Bambo's smile.

"I'm sorry." Kondi's heart thundered in her chest. She fell to the floor in exhaustion. "I didn't mean to hurt you, Bambo."

"Of course, you didn't." Bambo's hand gripped her shoulder. "I know that. But you did hit the right man—eventually." He smiled again and sat down beside her.

The room swarmed with officers now. Even so, Max leaped to his feet and dove between the feet of the policemen, trying to reach the doorway. Suddenly, an angry snarl sounded. A big dog rushed in and clamped his teeth over the back pocket of Max's pants, pinning the man to the ground.

Max screamed in pain. "Get the dog off me! No dogs! No dogs!"

Kondi's father pushed her out the door. She sank onto a nearby log and gasped for breath. "How did Ukhale get here?"

"Was that Ukhale?" Bambo sat down beside Kondi, still panting from his exertion. He swiped a hand over his face. "Ukhale, come!"

Ukhale appeared out of nowhere and sat down beside Bambo.

"Where's Ulemu?" Kondi swiveled around on the log looking for her friend.

"I don't know for sure," Bambo said. "Her father's also here somewhere. Perhaps she's with him."

"Ulemu!" Kondi stood up, looking into every corner of the clearing. "Mimi, where are you?"

"I'm here." Ulemu's soft voice came from behind

her. "I'm here with my father. I'm safe."

Kondi again sat down suddenly onto the log. She glanced around. Could that be Josi standing in the shadows? Of course, not. Surely he was at home, still weak from his illness.

Kondi jerked her arm away from a cold nudge. Ukhale nosed her arm up with his tongue lolling out of his mouth. He looked very pleased with himself. She reached to pat his head but the dog pulled away. He only allowed Josi to pet him.

"Thank you, God!" A shudder shook her whole body. She whispered this thankful prayer over and over as she began to cry.

About half an hour later, Bambo and Kondi walked into their *bwalo* at home and bent low to enter the cookhouse. Mai sat beside the fire. Kezo slept near her on a mat. A spiral of steam twisted from the spout of the teakettle Mai had kept hot. Both father and daughter sank onto stools near the fire and stared into the low flames.

Ulemu entered the cookhouse immediately behind them, but her father remained outside, not sure if he should come in.

"*Lowani*, Bambo Mbewe," Mai called. Ulemu's father peered through the doorway, then entered and squatted close to the doorway.

Kondi reached over and pushed one of the sticks

of firewood further under the teakettle, bringing its hum to a harder boil. "I'm relaxed for the first time in many days," she said.

"Yes." Bambo, and Mai said together.

"We've been worried about you, Kondi." Bambo ran a callused hand over his chin. "And Ulemu, too. But we knew this situation needed to be resolved, not just overlooked." He waved a hand toward Bambo Mbewe to include him in this decision.

Bambo Mbewe nodded solemnly.

"I'm sorry you were worried," Kondi said, "but I couldn't let Max hurt Kezo." She put her arm around Ulemu's shoulder. "I don't know how Max was making Mimi do what he wanted."

"Of course." The adults nodded their heads. "It was a strange situation to all of us."

Something rustled at the door. Kondi jumped up, her flight mode kicking in. Ukhale sat in the doorframe. A shaft of firelight poured from the kitchen, casting his shadow onto the hard-packed ground in the *bwalo* beyond. He knew better than to come into the cookhouse.

"Ukhale! Good dog!" Kondi reached a hand toward the dog, but he pulled back and went to lie down outside.

"Josi's the only one who's been able to make Ukhale a close companion," Mai said. "He protects our home, but he has only tolerated the rest of us."

"It's because Josi's the only one slipping him bites of food," Kondi teased, looking around to find him. But Josi wasn't there.

Bambo's chuckle began low in his chest. "It was so funny..." he gasped air "...to see that bad boy..." his chuckle built into a full roar of laughter..."get the dog bite he deserved!" Bambo swiped his forefinger and thumb over his eyes to brush away tears as he continued to laugh helplessly. The whole family and Bambo Mbewe joined in.

When they'd all settled down, Kondi said, "I thought I saw Josi with Ukhale at Max's camp. But how could he have been up there?"

"It *was* him, though." Ulemu's soft voice broke into a lull in the conversation. "I saw him, too."

The two girls looked around, but they couldn't find Josi in the kitchen or in the *bwalo*.

"Max may be a bad boy, as you say." Mai reached for the teakettle, set it off the fire, removed the lid and sprinkled tealeaves into it. "However, I'm sorry to see him in such trouble. He's lived a hard life."

"You have a kind heart to say so," Bambo said. "But many of us have not started life in an easy way, and have not done illegal things to get money for our support."

"Mmmm, it's true." Mai began to pour the tea. "Where *is* Josi, by the way?"

Just then, outside the doorway, the darkness stirred. Kondi's heart clenched.

"*Hodi*" someone called. It sounded like their friend from the police department. "May I come in by the fire?"

Mai beckoned him in, smiling and shaking her head at a man's ability to work his way into a

153

cookhouse. "I wouldn't want you to remain outside in the cold," she said, with a bit of sarcasm in her tone.

Policeman Banda bent to enter the low doorway. Josi followed him.

"Josi! There you are!" Mai said. "We were just asking about you."

"Josi played a very important role in our capture this evening," Policeman Banda said. "He and Ukhale. We didn't expect Josi and Ukhale to help. We couldn't have caught all three of these men without them. Ukhale pinned down one of Max's customers and my men caught the other one."

"That's wonderful!" Bambo exclaimed. "Then that *was* Ukhale up there at Max's camp! I thought the police must have started using dogs to help collar lawbreakers."

"Ukhale and Josi can join our police force any time," the policeman replied with a smile. "Without them this drug trafficker and his friends might have escaped tonight." He looked at Josi with a nod of approval.

"Why didn't you come home with us, Josi?" Kondi's frown showed her puzzlement.

"I wanted to know how the police would finish this case," he said. Josi's glance dropped to the mud floor of the kitchen house. "I just wanted to be there to help protect Kondi and Ulemu," he said. "And Ukhale followed me." He broke a twig into tiny bits and tossed the pieces into the fire. A smile of satisfaction crept across his features.

The group nodded with murmurs of approval. Mai began to hand around cups of tea.

"This 'bad boy' as you call him, Chisale," Policeman Banda said, "dealt not only in *chamba*. Marijuana selling's bad enough, but he also dealt in hard drugs. We found heroin, hallucinatory drugs, and even some cocaine in the boxes and packages at his camp." Their policeman friend shook his head. "It's a shame for such a young man to ruin his life. He may spend many years in prison if the courts declare him guilty. The evidence seems too strong for any other verdict."

"Kondi and Ulemu certainly did their part well," Josi said, breaking a moment of silence. He glanced at the girls huddled together near the fire. "I think Kondi and Ulemu were very brave to take those bad men to Max's camp. They helped much more than I did."

"Yes, of course." Policeman Banda nodded to the two girls. "Without their courageous help, we wouldn't have captured Max and his customers tonight. Those two buyers were his regular customers. They came over the border every two weeks to buy drugs from him."

"That's awful!" Kondi shook her head in dismay. "We *were* scared but we knew God went with us and we trusted the police to be there and Bambo to be right behind us, just as he'd said they all would be."

"Believing God would do what he said, and believing in a good man's word," Mai murmured. "That's faith at work."

They all sat silent for a bit, realizing how God had helped them during this frightening encounter.

"But why did you jump into the room ahead of the police, Chisale?" Policeman Banda broke into the silence. "You could have been killed."

"I just couldn't wait any longer. I wanted to protect the girls. I realize, now, it was a foolish thing to do." Bambo lowered his head with embarrassment. "Without God's help we would not have succeeded at all."

"Yes." Josi stood. "We should thank God in prayer, don't you think?"

"*Eya!*" Mai spoke for all the family as they stood together. Ulemu, Bambo Mbewe, and Policeman Banda joined them.

Bowing their heads, they each prayed silently for a few minutes and then Bambo said, "Thank you, God, for your protection tonight. Only you could give us success. Thank you for answering our prayers when we asked for protection. We give you glory for this victory, and we thank you that no one was hurt except the guilty persons." Their voices joined together in a resounding "Amen."

Kondi glanced around at those gathered by her. "I'm so blessed! I have a family I can trust. My parents love God. They led me to understand the truth about Max and to understand how God can bring me through hard times. I have great friends in Ulemu, Josi and Policeman Banda. God is good—all the time!"

Something moved just outside the door. They all

turned to see Ukhale sitting on his haunches in the fire's shaft of light. "Woof!" he said. His red tongue hung out the side of his mouth. He looked like he was smiling.

GLOSSARY

(Pronunciations are not given for English words)

Abambo anga (Ah′-bah-mboh ah′-ngah)
My father. A polite way to address one's father.

Agogo (Ah-go′-go)
Grandparents. The plural form is often used in speaking about one person, as a term of respect.

Bambo (Bah′mbo)
Father or Mr.

Bambo anga (bah′-mboh ah′-ngah)
My father.

Besom
A broom made of twigs for sweeping the yard.

Blind snake
A large worm that moves like a snake, but has no head.

Bwalo (Bwah′low)
Yard. It is hoed clean of grass to prevent snakes from coming near the house.

Bwerani (Bweh-rah′-nee)
Come as a command.

Chameleon
A slowly-creeping lizard-like creature. It hisses and it rolls its eyes around independently.

Chete (Cheh′-teh)
Be quiet.

Chigayo (Chee-gah′yo)
 A mill for grinding grain.
Chikondi (Chee-koh′-ndee)
 Joy, happiness--often used as a girl's name.
Chiyembekezo (Chee-yem-beh-keh′-zoh)
 Hope. Sometime used as a name.
Chirundu (Chee-roo′ndoo)
 A piece of cloth wrapped around the waist, used for a skirt, or to carry babies on the back, or to wrap around shoulders when cold. An extra one may be taken to market to carry home flour or grain.
Chipandi (Chee-pah′-ndee)
 A flat wooden spoon for serving up porridge patties.
Chiperoni (Chee-pay-roh′-nee)
 A cold, fine rain coming from over the Chiperoni Mountains.
Dambo (Dah′-mboh)
 A damp spot, usually at the base of a hill, where vegetables can be grown in the dry season.
Dedza (Deh′-dzah)
 A town in Malawi. It is about 50 miles south of Lilongwe, the capital city.
Eya (Eh-yah′)
 Yes.
Galimoto (Gah′-lee-moh-toh)
 Automobile.
Garner
 A small house for storing maize.

Gourd

A squash with a hard skin. Africans dry them and hollow them out for bowls and dippers.

Gogo (Goh'-goh)

Grandmother or grandfather.

Hodi (Hoh'-dee)

A word called at someone's yard or doorway indicating they want to enter.

Hoot

A British term meaning 'honk' often used in Malawi.

Hull

The outer skin of each maize kernel.

Iai (Ee-yah'-ee)

No.

Inde (Ee'-ndeh)

Yes.

Inde'di (Ee-ndeh'-dee)

Yes, indeed.

Iwe (Ee'-weh)

You. It is used to address children or as an insolent epithet to an adult.

Jacaranda (Jah-kah-rah'-nda)

A tall tree with lavender blossoms.

Kokoliko (Koh-koh-lee-koh)

The sound of a rooster's crow; cock-a-doodle-do.

Kondi (Koh'-ndee)

An abbreviation of Chikondi.

Kwacha (Kwah'-chah)

Freedom. Also their paper money.

Lowani (Loh-wah'-nee)
    Come in.
Lorry
    A large truck.
Madzi (Mah'-dzee)
    Water.
Mai (Mah'-ee)
    Mother or Mrs.
Mai-o! (Mah'-ee-oh)
    In moments of calamity, East and Central Africans often for their mothers.
Maize
    White field corn; a Malawian's main food.
Mandazi (Mah-ndah'-zee)
    A fried, donut-like pastry.
Mango (Mang'-goh)
    A tree bearing delicious tropical fruit.
Matalala (Mah-tah-lah'-lah)
    Hailstones
Machete (Mah-cheh-te)
    A huge, sharp knife used for slashing underbrush.
Mfiti (Mfee-tee)
    A witch or a wizard.
Mkeka (Mkeh'-kah)
    A finely woven grass mat.
Moni (Moh'-nee)
    Hello.
Moni-thu (Moh-nee'-too)
    Hello, indeed! (usually as a reply to someone's greeting)

Mortar

A heavy container hollowed out of a log, in which Africans pound grain.

Mwana'nga (Mwah-nah'-ngah)

My child

Ndine munthu'yo (Ndee'-nay moo-nthu'-yoh)

I am the person (the one you are looking for).

Ndine'yo (Ndee-nay'-yoh)

It is me (the one you are looking for).

Ndiwo (Ndee'-woh)

Any relish dish eaten with porridge.

Nsima (Nsee'-mah)

A very thick porridge made of maize meal, the staple of a Malawian's diet.

Nthali (Nthah'-lee)

A straight-sided pot for cooking porridge.

Nthiko (Nthee'-koh)

A wooden stirring paddle for stirring thick maize porridge.

Omen

A portent, a prophetic sign.

Pata-pata (Pah'-tah-pah'-tah)

Flip-flops; rubber sandals.

Pestle

The heavy pole used with the mortar to pound grain.

Pepani (Pay-pah'-nee)

Sorry.

Protea (Proh'-tee-yah)

A flowering bush of Eastern and Southern Africa.

Tambala (Tah-mbah'-lah)

Rooster. It is also the "cents" of their money system and a symbol of their freedom.

Ufa (Oo'-fah)

Maize flour.

Ukhale (Oo-khah'-lay)

Anger, ferocity. Often used for a dog's name.

Ulemu (Oo-leh'-moo)

Grace, courtesy. Sometimes used as a girl's name.

Yesu (Yay'-soo)

Jesus.

Zedi (Zeh'-dee)

Indeed. (Often abbreviated at the end of a word as "'di")

Zikomo (Zee-koh'-moh)

Thank you.

ABOUT THE AUTHOR

Sylvia Stewart grew up in the (then) Belgian Congo. She spent 21 years as an Assemblies of God missionary in Malawi, East Africa, with her husband, Duane. While there, she taught some writing workshops, which are now bearing fruit. She started writing Kondi's Quest hoping to weave a story for the children of Malawi.

In 1992 they were asked to go to Ethiopia to found a Bible College. They spent 11 years in Ethiopia doing mostly Bible College ministry. She taught college-level English to students who had never taken a grammar class before.

Sylvia has been published in Assemblies of God denominational magazines: *The Pentecostal Evangel* (now *Today's Pentecostal Evangel*); *Advance* (now *Enrichment*); *Woman's Touch*, and their missions magazine, *Mountain Movers*, which is no longer in print. She has also been published in *WASI Writer*, a writer's magazine published under the auspices of the University of Malawi.

Sylvia is the mother of four children, who grew up in Africa. Her eleven grandchildren are the delight of her life.

Printed in Great Britain
by Amazon